DRUG GANG TAKEDOWN

First published worldwide by System Addict Publishing in 2019

This edition published worldwide by System Addict Publishing in 2019

Copyright © Neil Walker 2019

All rights reserved. No part of this publication may be reproduced, distributed, or transmitted in any form or by any means, including photocopying, recording, or other electronic or mechanical methods, without the prior written permission of the publisher, except in the case of brief quotations embodied in critical reviews and certain other non-commercial uses permitted by copyright law.

This is a work of fiction. Names, characters, businesses, places, events and incidents are either the products of the author's imagination or used in a fictitious manner. Any resemblance to actual persons, living or dead, or actual events is purely coincidental.

NEIL WALKER

By the Same Author

Drug Gang

Drug Gang Vengeance: Drug Gang Part II

NEIL WALKER

For Louise

NEIL WALKER

Thanks to everyone who read the previous Drug Gang novels and spoke to me about them, either in person or through social media, or took the time to review them. Without your encouragement and desire to see the story continue, this book would not exist.

NEIL WALKER

CONTENTS

Chapter One	**19**
Chapter Two	**25**
Chapter Three	**31**
Chapter Four	**39**
Chapter Five	**47**
Chapter Six	**53**
Chapter Seven	**59**

Chapter Eight	**67**
Chapter Nine	**75**
Chapter Ten	**85**
Chapter Eleven	**93**
Chapter Twelve	**101**
Chapter Thirteen	**107**
Chapter Fourteen	**115**
Chapter Fifteen	**125**
Chapter Sixteen	**133**
Chapter Seventeen	**139**
Chapter Eighteen	**145**

Chapter Nineteen	**159**
Chapter Twenty	**165**
Chapter Twenty-One	**171**
Chapter Twenty-Two	**177**
Chapter Twenty-Three	**183**
Chapter Twenty-Four	**191**
Chapter Twenty-Five	**195**
Chapter Twenty-Six	**203**
Chapter Twenty-Seven	**209**
Chapter Twenty-Eight	**217**
Chapter Twenty-Nine	**225**

Chapter Thirty	**233**
Chapter Thirty-One	**241**
Chapter Thirty-Two	**249**
Chapter Thirty-Three	**257**
Chapter Thirty-Four	**263**
Chapter Thirty-Five	**269**
Chapter Thirty-Six	**279**
Chapter Thirty-Seven	**289**
Chapter Thirty-Eight	**295**
Chapter Thirty-Nine	**301**
Chapter Forty	**311**

"If you do not change direction, you may end up where you are heading."

Lao Tzu

DRUG GANG TAKEDOWN
Drug Gang Part III

NEIL WALKER

NEIL WALKER

Chapter One

Death, the end of everything, good and bad, joyful and painful, the great silence at the end of the cacophony and turmoil of life. John had been dicing with death for as long as he could remember, daring the Grim Reaper to kill him if he could. He'd always had a tendency to be quite self-destructive, with drugs, alcohol and the dangerous situations he would put himself in. In fact, he had come close to death before on a number of occasions.

On New Year's Eve in Manchester, with Simon bearing down on him with a circular saw and a large amount of sadistic delight, he'd thought it was all over and had made his peace with his own demise. He had seen death coming and accepted it - an end that's just in sight.

After surviving that night, as well as having come close to being killed in Sydney and perhaps even in Manchester the first time he was there, he had vowed to change his life and prioritise what was important.

Lisa - protecting her, loving her and being with her. That was what he deemed paramount. Good friends and family were significant too, but it had been Lisa who'd consumed his thoughts as he stared into the face of death, lying on the dance floor in The Casa nightclub on New Year's Eve.

How the hell had it come to this? He was supposed to get out. He was supposed to be out.

Sydney was meant to be a pit stop on the way to a fresh start. But again he'd compromised his plans, jeopardised what was important to him and had ended up once more on the floor, unable to escape, waiting to die.

They say anticipation of death is worse than death itself and as John knelt there, hooded and tied up on his knees, he could kind of see their point, whoever 'they' are.

He had been bound using cable ties. After a couple of years of tying people up with elephant tape, John could see the appeal. Cable ties were quick and easy to use, with less opportunity for the victim to struggle.

He couldn't see his watch, or anything else for that matter, but he imagined that around two hours had passed since he'd been bound and hooded. Two hours staring into the blackness of the inside of a cloth hood, waiting to die. Not knowing what was coming or when, but knowing that something unpleasant was on its way. This was cruel and unusual punishment.

He listened intently to any noise, bustling or snippets of conversation he could hear. To his right, he'd heard someone stripping and cleaning a .45 automatic pistol.

Despite his bleak situation and the prospect of worse to come, it amused him that he was able to identify this very specific process from sound alone. This was a testament to just how many times he'd done it himself.

So many people in the drug business didn't bother to correctly maintain their firearms, but John was a stickler for it. Proper cleaning and maintenance meant you could rely on a gun when you depended on it to save your life. In the wrong place at the wrong time, if the gun jams, you die.

He could actually strip and re-assemble a .45 automatic blindfolded. It was the kind of party trick that impressed people in the circles John had been moving in for the past couple of years.

On this occasion, he was effectively blindfolded, given that he could not see through the hood over his head, but he didn't imagine that his hosts would give him the opportunity to perform his famous party trick.

A .45 automatic pistol didn't hold enough bullets to shoot all of the people waiting to kill him anyway - although he would have liked the chance to try. John would sometimes surprise even himself with his ability to fight his way out of seemingly impossible scenarios.

This time it was the end though. It was game over. Life over.

There is no reset button in real life. No chance to go back to the start and have another go. Just death served cold by violent, sadistic animals, with no concept of mercy.

To them, kindness was seen as weakness, mercy was perceived as cowardice and negotiation was a code word for a bullet in the head.

In this moment, John was reminded of the Rage Against The Machine song 'Bullet in the Head'; the lyrics, 'You're brain dead, you've got a fuckin' bullet in your head.'

Although, John had read a couple of years previously that the lyrics of this song were actually a critique of the savvy propaganda of the initial Bush regime regarding The Gulf War, which the band viewed as an imperialist endeavour, rather than the song literally being about getting shot and receiving a bullet in your head.

It seemed to John that the song may as well have been about getting shot in the head, if the goal of the lyrics had been to alter people's perceptions and stop similar situations coming about again. George W. Bush, son of George H.W. Bush - who was President of the United States at the time of The Gulf War - had been in the White House since 2001 and he'd been busy leading a 'coalition of the willing' into a new war in Iraq, while John had been fighting a war of his own in Australia.

But while their war seemed to be just getting started, John's war was about to come to an end and he would soon be dead.

It would probably not be a bullet in the head that would actually kill him, however. This would no doubt be deemed too quick and easy an execution method for the great John Kennedy.

If he was lucky, they might finish him with a bullet in the head, after making him die badly for hours. Even that thought was John being optimistic about his prospects.

As he knelt there, tied and hooded on the floor, the credo from an addiction recovery coin that belonged to a friend of his in Belfast came to him and he repeated it in his head. 'Grant me the serenity to accept the things I cannot change, courage to change the things I can and wisdom to know the difference.'

The credo actually began with the word God on the coin: 'God grant me the serenity to accept the things I cannot change, courage to change the things I can and wisdom to know the difference', but John hadn't believed in God since he was a child and he wasn't going to start now, just because he was about to be killed.

Still, he agreed with the sentiment embossed on the coin and he needed to find the serenity to accept his situation, but could he use his courage to change anything? Did he have the wisdom to figure it out?

He was going to die in some horrific way, as were the rest of them. In their own way, they all had it coming; they were all in the game and they all knew the risks.

Not Lisa though. She didn't deserve any of this.

All she was guilty of was falling for the wrong guy and now she was going to die for it. Maybe he could bargain in some way; offer to play along with whatever they wanted, if they would spare her life. He would try if he got the chance, but he doubted he'd be successful.

Only a matter of weeks ago, they had been having the time of their lives in Hong Kong. Sydney was only supposed to be a brief layover on their way to an amazing new life. Instead, the chaos had caught up with John once again and consumed both him and Lisa.

Then he heard footsteps closing in on him - multiple sets of footsteps, stopping right beside him.

He felt two hands roughly pressing down on his shoulders and another hand grabbing the top of the cloth hood that was over his head, ready to pull it off. They had come for him.

Now it was time to die.

Chapter Two

Bruce Lee had always been a kind of hero and role model to John, in the absence of a father figure, someone to look up to and emulate.

He had always intended to study up on the martial art created by Bruce Lee, which is called Jeet Kune Do. Inspired by the fact that he would be stopping over in Hong Kong, where Bruce Lee was raised and where he first found fame, he had purchased the book The Tao of Jeet Kune Do in Belfast before he and Lisa had left on their travels.

The fact that their stopover in Hong Kong had now extended to over four weeks meant that he'd had plenty of time to read, study and memorise the content of this iconic book. He didn't turn over a page of the book until he had physically practiced and mastered the techniques contained on the pages in front of him and committed the contents to memory.

It had been a difficult start to 2003, with John needing several weeks to recover from the damage he sustained in Manchester during his battle with The Brotherhood on New Year's Eve. Even after he had healed up, he still had to look after Blair in Belfast, until Blair was fit to travel back to Australia.

From the moment Lisa arrived at Belfast International Airport to meet him, however, John had begun enjoying life again and he and Lisa were making the most of every second in Hong Kong.

There was a gym high up in a skyscraper that he and Lisa would work out in most days, but that was largely fitness and weights training. John would also do around an hour and a half of combat training in the hotel room in the early evening, before he and Lisa would head out to dinner. This gave the room a chance to air out, while John and Lisa were out for food and drinks, after John's sweaty exercise regime.

They both enjoyed walking around Victoria Harbour, especially Lisa. Every time John was down there, he would hear the theme music from Enter The Dragon playing in his head, and his fondness for Hong Kong movies meant that being there gave him a particular kind of special buzz.

For Lisa, it was more about clearing her head and the inner peace that can be found in the moments of staring out at the water and watching the boats and the people. She would usually walk around the harbour by herself, while John did his combat training in the hotel room.

They had got into a pretty pleasant and comfortable routine during their time in Honkers, as the locals would often call it.

Their long stay had given John the opportunity to train his way right through The Tao of Jeet Kune Do and he was currently working on the last couple of combat sections in the book: attack by combination and attack by drawing. There was a full-length mirror in the hotel room, which made it ideal for this kind of work out.

A lot of the strikes, moves, footwork and combinations in the book John was already familiar with, having trained in western boxing, Thai boxing and Judo. In particular, there were a lot of western boxing elements used in Jeet Kune Do. Nevertheless, it was Bruce Lee's unique way of looking at the techniques, fusing them together and giving his own individual view and philosophy on how to use them that John found hugely beneficial.

As well as perfecting his moves in front of the full-length mirror, John would stare at the bizarre piece of artwork hanging up in the room as he trained. It was a highly unusual painting of a group of what looked like bodybuilding teddy bears, marching together in line. The painting resembled something from a creepy horror film; John loved it. Lisa was not quite so keen.

John would also gaze out the window at their magnificent view, almost as much as he would stare at the sinister teddy bear painting.

He couldn't get over the fact that bamboo scaffolding was used to build skyscrapers in Hong Kong, or the way that high-end buildings - such as fancy hotels and business towers - often stood side by side with slum apartment buildings. It was a unique and intoxicating place.

The default music in the CD player the whole time they had been there was a compilation Lisa had made before they left. This compilation was being played in the room on a daily basis.

It was made up entirely of songs by artists from Northern Ireland. This included well-known acts like Ash, Therapy? and The Undertones, as well as more obscure bands like Watercress, The Serranos and Joyrider. Maybe it was her way of bringing a piece of home with her.

The CD was a great, although the volume was a bit inconsistent between some tracks. Even though John was a fan of the songs and artists on this compilation, it had become completely played out for him in the four weeks they had been in Honkers. He felt like if he heard 'Summertime With Me' by Watercress or 'Just In Sight' by The Serranos one more time, he would scream - or at the very least slam his finger down hard on the stop button of the CD player.

They were just using a personal CD player, plugged into some small portable speakers. With the volume up high, there was a decent sound level coming out of it.

When Lisa was out, John always changed the disc in the CD player and today's choice was 'The Doors' album by The Doors. For John's money, The Doors eponymous debut was one of the greatest albums of all time. Although it was not perfect training music, he did his best to make it suit his purpose - programming the CD player to play the slower tunes for the warm up and warm down and the more up tempo tracks for the main workout.

As John neared the end of his exercise session and was getting ready to warm down, his thoughts turned to his mobile phone. Lisa had suggested they both switch off their mobiles when they got to Hong Kong and just leave them in the safe, making the pair of them untouchable to the world at large. John had agreed and in the weeks they'd been there, neither of them had checked their phones or even switched them on.

Now that they were finally considering leaving for their next destination of Sydney, John was wondering if there'd been any contact from Blair during their month of self-imposed exile in Honkers.

How had Blair been getting on running the Sydney drug gang? Was everything in place for John to pick up his money and get on with his fresh start? Could they both now move on and begin their new life together - he and Lisa?

As he stretched his body to warm down, while listening to 'The End' by The Doors, John could hold off his curiosity no longer.

He crossed the room, removed his mobile phone from the safe and switched it on. As the phone lit up and became functional, it quickly buzzed with a backlog of nine new text-messages. When John clicked through them, he could see that they were all from Blair. Something was going on - that much was clear.

John selected the last and most recent text-message and opened it up. It contained only two words: 'It's war.'

Chapter Three

Blair had quickly managed to establish himself as the new leader of the Sydney drug gang. The fact that he had effectively been joint number two in the gang since its early days had made this a relatively easy and seamless transition, especially given that the former boss, John, had stepped down and the other previous joint number two, Peter, had been killed by John in Manchester.

Things had gone smoothly for the first couple of weeks, but then the violent incidents began. It seemed that a turf war was brewing, although Blair was yet to get confirmation of exactly who the competition were.

O'Neill's Bar was an old and dying pub; the number of patrons had been falling year on year for a while and the owner, Harry, had been getting ready to cut his losses before Blair approached him. Harry had not been hard to convince, given the dire financial predicament in which he found himself and his bar.

Blair was able to use the pub to tally up with his dealers on club nights, cut up drugs and count money in the back room, launder money through the books, have any necessary business meetings in the bar or out the back, as well as just having a quiet bar to have a drink in whenever he liked. In return, Harry got paid very well.

At the end of the day, business is about money and Harry could see that this was his only appealing fiscal option. Plus, Harry was a nice, affable guy and even though he was deep into middle age, with greying hair and a growing waist line, he had a good rapport with the young drug dealers, who were all in their early to mid-twenties.

The bar itself was nothing special; it was small, narrow, dark and hadn't been decorated in a long time. Most people had forgotten it was even there and would walk past it.

For Blair's purposes, it was perfect.

The only thing about O'Neill's Bar that wasn't ideal for Blair was the music. Blair loved techno and saw it as the perfect music for all occasions. Any music that he liked from other genres he still only viewed as just alright and he would've loved to have techno playing in the bar at all times.

Harry liked classic rock n' roll, mostly from the nineteen sixties, seventies and eighties. He would put five discs in the stereo CD changer, set them to shuffle and leave them to play all night through the PA system.

Tonight there were albums by The Beatles, The Rolling Stones, The Who, The Kinks and Crowded House.

Like a lot of Australians, Blair did like Crowded House and was enjoying the track 'Everything Is Good For You' as it played out through the pub. His lieutenant, Nate, was even singing along with it, as they sat in their usual spot at the back corner table of the bar. Blair was not singing along, as the song was not techno and was therefore just alright.

Nate had been one of Blair's guys in the drug gang, when he was a lieutenant and John was in charge. Nate was twenty-three - a few years older than Blair - and had stood out as Blair's toughest and smartest guy in the past.

He was tall and well built, so he looked intimidating. Also, he was well trained up in several martial arts and tended to be able to fight his way out of any situation that he couldn't think or talk his way out of.

He was the obvious choice for promotion when Blair took over as gang leader and had proved to be an excellent lieutenant.

Every club night, Nate would sit with Blair in the back corner of O'Neill's Bar and wait for the gang members to stop in for a drink and to make a cash drop from their night's drug dealing. They would be sat there from around midnight until close to dawn.

On this particular Saturday night, it was just after midnight and Blair and Nate hadn't been in O'Neill's Bar for long. None of the dealers had called in to make cash drops yet and the bar was deserted, apart from Blair, Nate and Harry.

Harry was polishing glasses and tidying up the bar, as he nodded his head in time with 'Everything Is Good For You'. Blair and Nate were sipping their first Hahn Light of the night, savouring the cold beer in their designated corner of the bar, where they liked to conduct business.

The sound and motion of the front door swinging abruptly open caught all of their attention at the same time.

As the figure emerged through the doorway, Harry spun his head to look at Blair and Nate, immediately recognising the notorious individual who was entering his precious pub and showing his concern with the expression on his face.

As the man walked into the bar, Blair and Nate quickly recognised him as well. He was more than a little familiar to them.

This man walked with a limp, had a severe looking scar on his face and was sporting a trench coat. He was carrying a brown paper bag in his right hand, which he held in the air as he made his way through the bar towards Blair and Nate. It was Hatchet Willis.

Hatchet Willis was a well-known face in Australia; although his face had only had the gruesome scar added to it about six months previously.

His criminal exploits had become the stuff of legend in Australia as a whole and particularly in Sydney.

He was in his thirties and very much looked it. He'd had a tough life and it showed. He had a shaved head and a number of prison style tattoos, mostly hidden by his trench coat at this point, which he had of course largely got while serving time in prison.

Even with his trench coat on, the tattoo on his neck was visible: the words 'Kill 'Em All' in black ink, written in a way that made it look like they'd been done with an ordinary needle. The tattoos on his knuckles were also visible and consisted of a word on each hand, written in the same style as the tattoo on his neck: the words were, 'FUCK' and 'YOU!'

His gang, The Hatchet Mob, were both feared and revered and were known to use extreme violence to gain and protect their territory.

When John was still leader of the Sydney drug gang that was now headed by Blair, he'd taken on Hatchet Willis and his two lieutenants in the gents toilets of Spice nightclub and had violently injured all three of them.

Both the scar on Willis' face and the limp in his step were the results of the brutally violent lesson John had taught them.

John had thought he'd done enough in the men's bathroom in Spice, on that particular night, to scare off The Hatchet Mob and keep them out of his gang's territory in future. It now looked like he had been wrong.

The Hatchet Mob had stayed away for a while, but had apparently come back for what they believed was theirs.

It seemed the mystery of who'd been instigating a turf war with Blair's gang had been solved. The Hatchet Mob appeared to want a war with them and Hatchet Willis was presenting himself to Blair for reasons that were as yet unclear.

Nate did not hesitate, once he realised that Hatchet Willis had entered the pub. He quickly pulled out the .22 automatic they kept stuffed down between the L shaped leather bench style seats of their business corner of the bar.

This pistol was kept on hand for if and when they needed it, but was small and well hidden enough that it would be unlikely to be seen or detected if there was a surprise visit from the police.

Nate stood up with the gun in his hand, aiming it at Willis as he slowly limped towards them. Blair remained seated, but was alert and ready to act.

Did Hatchet Willis want to talk, or was O'Neill's Bar about to erupt into violence and bloodshed?

Hatchet Willis smiled at the pair of them as he got closer and was completely unfazed by Nate pulling the gun. As he arrived at their corner of the pub, he placed the brown paper bag he had with him on the bar and turned to face Blair and Nate, standing in front of their table.

Blair and Nate were tense and ready for action, while Willis seemed incredibly relaxed, especially considering he had a gun pointed at him.

Initially, Blair and Nate didn't say anything, but Willis was happy to break the ice.

"G'day guys, how are you goin'?"

Chapter Four

Hatchet Willis leaned back nonchalantly against the bar of the virtually deserted pub, looking across at Blair and Nate, waiting for a reaction to his greeting. Nate continued to stand silently, aiming his gun at Willis' head.

Blair did his best not to seem rattled, and addressed this rival gang boss.

"G'day Willis, or should I call you Hatchet?"

"Willis is fine Blair; I'm not big on formality."

Hatchet Willis had casually let Blair know that he knew who he was and it had not been lost on him. He didn't react or ask him how he knew though.

Willis was playing it very cool and Blair would do his best to emulate this behaviour.

"Do you want to tell your man Nate to lower that little bloody peashooter? He might accidentally let one go, eh."

Both Blair and Nate made a mental note that he knew both their names.

He also blatantly knew what time and on what day to find them in O'Neill's Bar and no doubt what they used it for. Just how much did The Hatchet Mob know about their operation?

There was little time for them to ponder this question, as Willis held his trench coat open to reveal no guns and no knives or hatchets in the loops on the inside of the coat. Based on what John had told him from his encounter with Hatchet Willis and The Hatchet Mob the previous year in Spice nightclub, Blair knew that these loops would usually be loaded with weapons, so it appeared he had come in peace.

"Put the gun down mate," Blair instructed Nate.

Nate lowered his weapon, but kept it in his hand.

At this point, Harry felt it was the appropriate time to interject with a reasonable request.

"Do you guys mind taking it out the back?"

Willis didn't turn or react, but Blair nodded to Harry, before directing Willis towards the door to the back room with a wave of his right hand.

"This way mate."

Nate still had his gun held low to his right side and was looking on with curiosity, as Willis picked up the brown paper bag he'd brought in with him from the bar. It was clear that the bag was well filled with something and Hatchet Willis carried it with him.

"What's in the bag?" asked Nate, as they made their way towards the door to the back room. It was making him nervous and he felt he had to ask.

"Oh, I brought you guys a little peace offering. Something to get stuck into."

This reply from Willis, combined with the fact that he was now starting to smell the feint aroma of Chinese food, was enough to relax Nate on the issue. Blair hadn't been as concerned as Nate about the brown paper bag contents, as he felt that if Willis was there for a fight, he'd probably have come in mob-handed and guns blazing. The carnage would have already begun.

An eerie sense of menace filled the dimly lit back room of O'Neill's Bar, as Hatchet Willis, Blair and Nate sat down facing each other around the large round table in the centre of it. It was as if they were sitting down for a game of poker, with their lives as the stake.

All three of them were watching each other closely and were very much on their guard as they took their seats, before Willis began taking out rectangular foil containers, with white cardboard lids on top of them, from the brown paper bag.

He placed five of them in the middle of the table and pulled out chopsticks and plastic knives and forks. He then picked up one of the containers and a set of chopsticks, opened the container and began eating some chicken fried rice.

Blair and Nate looked on, not ready to start eating yet themselves, before Willis began talking - with his mouth full.

"I'm just here to talk fellas. You won't have to pull out that little Desmond Two-Two again and open up on me."

Willis was smiling as he spoke.

"Hit me a few times with that bloody thing you might hurt me."

Both Blair and Nate couldn't help but snigger at this witty remark, before putting their life and death poker faces back on.

"What exactly do you want to talk about mate?" asked Blair.

"Seems like my guys and your guys have been having a spot of bother," explained Willis, still throwing chicken fried rice into his mouth with the chopsticks. "Thought we'd best sit down and thrash it out, eh."

There was a brief pause before Blair asked, "Oh yeah, what do you suggest?"

"I suggest we have a chat about it Blair, me old mate. Why don't you two dig in to the grub and we'll see what's what?"

Blair and Nate reached into the middle of the table for the four remaining foil cartons, taking two each. Willis continued talking and eating.

"So, we've been bumping heads a little bit and there's been some of the old rough stuff. It's not good for business."

"Too right it's not," agreed Blair, as he opened up his first container. It contained a Peking style chicken noodle dish that Blair nodded his approval at.

Nate opened his first container to reveal a salted chilli chicken dish, which was also to his liking.

"It seems to me there have been a few clubs that we overlap on and where the disturbances keep happening. The big one is Spice," Willis continued, as Blair and Nate took a first bite of food from their respective containers, each opting to use a plastic fork rather than chopsticks.

"We all know how much money there is to be made knocking out a bit of gear in Spice and there's gonna be serious trouble if we don't reach an agreement on it."

Blair nodded at him with his mouth full, as he took the lid off his second foil container. As he peeled off the white cardboard lid, he was aghast at what he saw inside.

He jumped back in his seat, spitting out what food remained in his mouth. Nate noticed him do this, just as he too took the white cardboard lid off his second foil container and was also horrified by the contents.

Each foil dish contained a severed human hand, stewing in its own blood.

"Sorry boys, I wasn't sure how you take them," Willis joked. "I like mine rare, with a bit of blood."

"What the fuck?" was all Blair could muster as a response.

"I thought I'd make it simple for ya. You see, those couple of hands belong to a couple of your boys who thought they could deal in Spice tonight. It turns out they got it wrong."

Hatchet Willis had a self-satisfied smirk on his face.

"I used the old hatchet to take their hands off - just one hand each mind you, and their left ones at that. I'm not a cruel guy by nature."

"Are they alive?" asked Blair, concerned that Willis had killed as well as mutilated his two friends and fellow gang members.

"Ah, they'll be right. A couple of the boys dropped them near the hospital. I told them not to let them bleed out."

"You sick fucker," chimed in Nate.

"Yeah," a grinning Willis agreed.

Nate reached for the .22 automatic he had tucked into his trousers and aimed it at Willis' head. Blair quickly reached across the table for his arm, just managing to hit it with the palm of his hand as Nate pulled the trigger.

A shot whistled just past the head of Hatchet Willis, who barely flinched and never stopped smiling.

"Put it away mate," Blair ordered Nate.

"That's right mate, put it away," agreed Willis. "You see, there's a fuckin' bunch of nasty cunts waiting for me outside; nasty cunts who work for me - Hatchet Mob cunts. If I don't come out alive, no one in here does."

Blair and Nate both took this on board and Nate tucked the gun back into his trousers.

"Well, I think that'll do, eh."

Willis slid his chair back, as he prepared to stand up.

"I think we're all clear here. That's just a little warning, but if I catch any of your guys in any of my clubs again, I might just lose my temper."

Willis got to his feet, picking up his partially consumed container of chicken fried rice and his chopsticks from the table. He then made his way to the door, continuing to eat the Chinese food.

Before he left through the door, he made one final remark.

"Eat up boys. Don't let it go to waste."

Hatchet Willis left the back room of the pub, closing the door behind him.

Blair and Nate sat there in stunned silence for a few seconds, before Blair reached into his pocket for his mobile phone. He pulled it out and began sending a text-message.

"What are we gonna do mate?" asked Nate.

"The first thing I'm gonna do is text John."

"Again?"

"Yes mate, again. Things have got a little bit more urgent and of all the gangsters I'd like at my side for this, he's gangster number one."

"What are you gonna text him?"

"It's war."

Chapter Five

`Hong Kong by night was an awe-inspiring sight of neon majesty. It was the kind of breathtaking cityscape that lit up like a living work of art.

John could have stared at it for hours and indeed had done many times, since he and Lisa had been there. On this occasion, he had just been gazing out at the stunning spectacle through the hotel window for a few minutes, as he waited for Lisa to return.

Having finished his workout, showered and got himself ready to go out for dinner, there was nothing left for him to do but enjoy the view, listen to some music and think of what he was going to say to Lisa when she got back.

Their hotel room was on the thirty-seventh floor and the elevated perspective they had was incredible. The first time John had seen this view by night, he couldn't get over how much Hong Kong looked like Blade Runner.

John was a huge fan of the movie Blade Runner, especially since he had seen the Director's Cut. He was now sure that Ridley Scott must have been inspired by Hong Kong to create the look of the futuristic sci-fi world depicted in the film.

In keeping with staring into this illuminated, futuristic cityscape, John had selected the album 'Moon Safari' by Air as the background music. He wasn't really concentrating on the CD though, as he was far too focussed on how he was going to tell Lisa about his breach of their mobile phone agreement and the information he had discovered, now that he'd checked his text-messages.

While John and Lisa had been spanning time and rejuvenating in Honkers, things had been going crazy in Sydney.

Blair was an intelligent and capable guy, but it seemed he badly needed John's help. A war had been brewing and it was about to escalate out of control.

As far as John was concerned, he was out. He was not a drug dealer any more and he was out of the violent drug world.

The weeks in Hong Kong had been all the more enjoyable with this thought in his head; the idea he would never again sell drugs or be involved in the vicious conflicts that are part and parcel of drug dealing. He absolutely did not want to get drawn back into the unpleasant world he had just managed to get himself out of.

He'd hoped that they would just arrive in Sydney, he would get the money Blair owed him, pick up a few things and take care of arrangements for his Sydney apartment. Then he and Lisa could be on their way; travelling the world as international, globe-trotting lovers.

He felt a huge sense of obligation to Blair, however. When John needed him, Blair had put his life in Sydney on hold and travelled to Belfast, then to Manchester to help him. He had risked his life and almost lost it.

John knew that he owed Blair. Although the sense of obligation he felt would not be lost on Lisa, John doubted she would react well to the situation.

He turned from the view of the Hong Kong night, as the door opened behind him and Lisa emerged through it, with a smile on her face and a couple of shopping bags in her hands.

She set them down on the ground near the door and let the door slam shut behind her.

"Okay, so I may have got a little carried away. It's all essentials though," she joked.

"What did you get me?" John joked back.

Lisa reached down into one of the shopping bags with her right hand and then pulled the hand out again with the middle finger extended and gestured it at John, giggling as she revealed it.

"There you go. That's all for you," she announced.

John laughed, but was mindful that things were about to get serious.

"I know I'm running late, but I just need a quick shower, I'll throw on a dress and we can go and eat. I am starving."

"Sounds good. Just one thing I have to tell you first."

"Okay, quickly. I'm sweating here."

"Horses sweat, men perspire and women glow," John laughingly corrected.

"Very good," said Lisa, chuckling. "Seriously though, what is it? I could eat a horse right now, let alone sweat like one."

"Alright. So, you know the way we said we'd keep our mobile phones off until we were leaving?"

"Yes."

"Well, we're going to be leaving soon anyway, so I turned mine on and took a peek."

"John, we agreed."

"I know, I'm sorry."

"Anything to report?"

"I had nine text-messages, all from Blair."

"What did he want?" asked Lisa, the concern obvious in her voice.

"He's in trouble Lisa. Things are kicking off in Sydney and he needs my help."

"No way John. You said you were retired from all that bollocks."

"I know, but I owe him Lisa. He risked his life for me. He risked his life for you."

"Oh no! Don't fucking do that! I'm not going to let you make me feel guilty about this."

"Okay Lisa, but I do feel like I owe Blair."

"Blair has been a good friend to you, but that doesn't mean you have to go to Sydney and jump right back into the old madness."

"I know babe, I don't want to get back in. I was just thinking I could help him out for a while and make sure he's okay."

"Help him out? John, if you are thinking about going and running around Sydney with a gun again, I'm going home. I never would have come with you if I'd thought you weren't finished with all that shit."

"Actually, I prefer to run around with two guns," John responded, hoping to lighten the mood.

Lisa couldn't help but laugh a little, but then added, "I'm serious John. Now I'm going for a shower."

Lisa disappeared into the bathroom, having made her point of view perfectly clear.

John knew that she meant what she said and, in a lot of ways, he knew she was right. Getting involved in the drug war in Sydney would obviously be a bad idea and, despite the sense of obligation he felt to Blair, he couldn't risk losing Lisa.

Plus, after everything he had put Lisa through and everything that had happened to them the last time they were in Sydney because of him, he couldn't fight her on this.

And he absolutely did not want to risk her leaving his life. She was the only thing he really cared about at this point.

What was he going to tell Blair though? Blair had followed him around the world, seemingly without a second thought, to risk his life and help him, out of loyalty.

Could John really look him in the eye and tell him that he would not help him fight the drug war in Sydney?

Chapter Six

It was autumn in Australia, but the temperature, as John and Lisa sat outside a cafe in Darling Harbour, was around twenty-three degrees Celsius. It was a glorious sunny day, warmer than most summer days in Belfast. Lisa had been able to wear a light summer dress and John was wearing an Everlast t-shirt and cargo shorts.

Darling Harbour was a beautiful and picturesque place to sit outside, have a drink and soak up the sun. There were a number of cafes and bars with al fresco areas so people could choose to take a table out in the air and look at the water and across the harbour. There was even a ship that had been reconditioned as a restaurant, which was a place John had always meant to try but had never got round to it.

Lisa was enjoying an iced frappe, while John was making do with a soda water and lime. He had wanted Pepsi, or at the very least Coca-cola, but the waitress had informed him that they did not serve cola.

This was clearly quite a pretentious place, but it had a free table outside with a great view, so John had let the cola issue go and made do.

As they sat there people watching, a guy walked by wearing a grey t-shirt that sported a motto in large white letters: 'HAVE NO REGRETS'. John was instantly struck by the irony of this regrettable t-shirt choice, although he did agree with the sentiment it proclaimed to a certain extent.

Carrying the past around with you like a burden on your shoulders is unhealthy; but you have to learn from the past before you let it go. When you lose, don't lose the lesson.

John and Lisa's last few days in Hong Kong had been marred a little by the atmosphere that had remained between the two of them after John broke their agreement about checking their mobile phones. A certain amount of ill feeling and awkwardness had lingered after the reading of Blair's texts and their conversation about them. Lisa was clearly on edge and concerned that John might end up going back to his old ways.

John had only text-messaged Blair back to let him know when they were arriving in Sydney and to arrange to meet him. They had agreed to meet in Darling Harbour, so they could enjoy the scenery and the weather. Also, Darling Harbour wasn't too far from John's Sydney apartment.

John and Lisa had spent a great morning wandering around Sydney.

The pair of them had done the walk they always used to enjoy together: through the park and up to the lookout, which gives you a great view of Sydney Opera House.

On the way up to the lookout, they had seen a number of locals and backpackers using inflated, empty wine bags, from the inside of wine boxes, as sunbathing pillows. Lisa was amused when John informed her that some Australians referred to these shiny silver bags as goon bags, and that buying cheap boxes of wine, taking out the inner bag, drinking the wine through the little plastic tap and then inflating the bag to use as a pillow was a very common practice in Australia, particularly among young people.

He'd been told that the word goon was the Aboriginal word for pillow and that the practice had originated in the Aboriginal community, although he wasn't sure if this was true. When he explained this to Lisa, she seemed to enjoy hearing the snippet of trivia. John had spent a lot more time than her living in Australia and had a better overall knowledge of the country.

Beside the bench at the lookout, some children had hung a rope and a tyre from the branch of a tree to make a rope swing. John informed Lisa that this had been one of his favourite childhood pastimes in Belfast, as well as climbing up on rooves protected by barbed wire, jumping off those rooves and setting on fire anything that would burn.

Lisa pointed out that he and his friends from the estate would possibly have benefited from a leisure centre when growing up. This had tickled them both.

After sitting on the bench, looking out at the view and talking for a while, they had walked out of the park and made their way to an internet cafe, where they had spent a couple of hours getting up to date on news and their emails on two computers side by side, with John also making a point of checking the Middlesbrough Football Club website for results and updates.

Internet cafes were a huge thing in Australia. They were always busy and made plenty of money, charging a rate per fifteen minutes of internet use.

After the Internet cafe, they had got a milkshake and then walked down to Sydney Opera House, managing to get one of the concrete lookout benches at the front of it, by the water. This is where they would have sometimes come at night - when they lived in Sydney - and just sat there talking or looking out at the dark blanket of water, trying to spot shark fins.

It had been a memorable and highly nostalgic day, which they'd both enjoyed. Now it was time to get serious, however. It was time to talk money, business and war.

Blair held out his arms as he walked up in front of them and greeted them loudly.

"Sun's out, cunts out!"

They both laughed and stood up to hug and greet him. Having done this, the three of them all sat down at the table.

"So, how are you guys going? Good flight?"

"Yeah, it wasn't too bad. I think we're both just a bit tired now," responded Lisa, taking the lead in the small talk and also letting it be known that she didn't want this business discussion to go on for too long.

"Weather's awesome isn't it?"

"I can't believe it. And this is your autumn," pointed out Lisa.

"Yeah, the weather in Sydney in April is great. I suppose this is your first April down under?"

"Yeah."

"So anyway guys, check this out," said Blair, standing up and fidgeting with his metal belt buckle.

He popped the front of it and it unfolded to reveal a small knife, which had been concealed within the buckle, obviously designed for self-defence.

"How cool is that?"

Lisa did not respond to this question, but John did, giving his genuine opinion.

"That is so fucking cool mate."

"You want a drink Blair, or will I just go and pay the bill?" asked Lisa.

"I'm good thanks," answered Blair.

Lisa went into the cafe to pay the bill. In Belfast, she would have just asked for the it to be brought over and left the money on the table, but even in her brief time in Australia previously, she had seen people snatching money left on tables like this and running away with it. Apparently it was a problem in Australia, especially in Sydney.

As Lisa made her way inside, John took the opportunity to get his first business update from Blair.

"How is everything mucker?"

"It went off big time last night mate. They hit us everywhere. Guns, knives, hatchets, machetes - it was nuts. The cops are going bloody crazy."

"Seriously, that bad?"

"Yeah John. This is bigger than anything we've ever dealt with. It's getting out of control. Sydney is turning into a fucking war zone."

Chapter Seven

Lisa was in the bedroom, with the door closed, going through her stuff, deciding what she needed to keep and bring with her and what she needed to get rid of. Despite the closed door, Blair and John made their way out on to the balcony of John's open plan apartment, for an extra layer of privacy.

The three of them had walked back to the apartment together from Darling Harbour, stopping for lunch in a Thai restaurant along the way. The conversation had flowed along well enough, although it had been slightly stilted by the huge elephant in the room: namely the drug war that was going on, Blair's text-messages to John about it and his intention to try to get John involved.

Now that they were back at the apartment and Lisa was otherwise occupied, allowing John and Blair to discuss these issues more freely, it was time to get to it.

After a quick check that the surrounding balconies were clear, they sat down on the two metal chairs at either side of the small metal table that furnished the balcony and got down to business.

"So mate, where do we start?" asked Blair.

Although the obvious starting point was the previous night's bloodshed, John wanted to clarify his money situation before discussing the war and inevitably disappointing Blair. He was fairly confident that Blair wouldn't be petty about the money, even if he did feel let down by John, but he thought it best to be sure.

"At the risk of sounding like a greedy cunt, we could start by talking about my money."

Blair grinned and nodded.

"I get you mate; you've got to look after yourself and Lisa, make sure you both come out okay. Don't worry John, I'll look after you."

"So what's the story?"

"I've got your money for you and you've got two options. You can have it in cash, in a case, like literally as soon as I can get it to you, or you can have it washed and in an account."

"Washed sounds good. How long would that take and what's the hit?"

Blair smiled before replying, noting how quickly John had worked the angles in his head and covered them in his answer.

"It would take a few days and it costs you twenty cents on the dollar."

Blair paused, to let John take on board the price tag, before continuing his explanation.

"For that, you get clean money in an offshore account with all the cards and paperwork you'll need. All untraceable."

John thought for a few seconds before replying.

"It's a little steep, but worth it. Let's put a wash on."

Blair laughed, before getting to the part of the conversation he was primarily interested in.

"Now that we've sorted out your financials, let's talk about last night's citywide butchery and the huge bloody drug war we've got going on."

"How bad was last night?"

"They hit us everywhere, mob-handed. It was carnage. Chris is dead. A few of the other guys are badly hurt; they should survive though."

"Chris? Fucking hell. I always liked Chris; he was a good guy. How did he die?"

"Meat cleaver through the fucking skull."

"Fuck me!"

"At least it was quick," said Blair, in a resigned tone.

"And it was The Hatchet Mob?"

"Yeah, Hatchet Willis cut off a couple of the boys' hands last week and brought them to me with a warning."

"Jesus."

"I guess this is what happens when you don't listen to his warnings."

"So he told you to stand your gang down from dealing; that he was claiming all your clubs, all your turf?"

"He only said Spice and a couple of other clubs that he sees as being his. I guess I made it worse by ignoring him."

John took a moment to let this sink in.

"The Hatchet Mob hit you in six clubs, mob-handed, on the same night, because you defied them on three places?"

"Yeah, all at the same time."

"I didn't think they had that kind of manpower."

"Old Willis must have been recruiting; big time. He looks lovely by the way, with that bloody big scar on his face and a fucking limp."

John stifled a laugh, realising that, if anything, he had made the Hatchet Mob situation worse with his extreme actions in Spice the previous year, giving Hatchet Willis his facial scar and limp.

"I need you man," confessed Blair.

"Blair, you know I want to help you. I know you need me and I know I owe you. But I promised Lisa."

"Even if you just strap up for a week or two and we run them out of our clubs, I think that could put a lid on it."

"I can't strap up mate. I'll help you in any other way I can, but I can't go back to getting blood on my hands. Not after I promised Lisa and after what happened to her before because of me."

Blair understood where John was coming from, but he was desperate, caught up in a drug war he didn't think he could win.

"Please John."

"Blair, you've got so many guys and guns, ways and means. Why do you need me?"

"You're lightning in a bottle John. I know I can win it if I've got you in the trenches with me."

"Mate, I would love to help you, I really would. I know how much you've helped me and I appreciate everything you've risked. I've got my hand in the knickers over the whole thing."

"Hand in the knickers; what do you mean?"

"I feel a cunt."

They both laughed.

As the laughter subsided, Blair took a more serious and sincere tone.

"You know mate, when I was recovering for all that time in your bedroom in Belfast, I had nothing much to do but read and watch TV. I read a ton of your philosophy books, as well as watching a load of your videos."

"Yeah, I remember. Every time I'd come back into the room, you'd have your nose in one of my books."

"Yes mate and I learned a lot. And one of the many things I learned is that the job of your life is to know yourself. It's the hardest job you'll ever do. Who are you really John? To thine own self be true."

John understood what Blair was getting at, but chose instead to pick up on how far Blair had come philosophically and in his outlook on life, in a very short time.

"Fucking hell Blair, you really did get a lot out of those books. I remember as recently as Christmas time last year, you were seeing the world in very simple terms; everything was black and white. You were buying into the old-fashioned idea of good and evil; drop an O from the first word, add a D to the second - God and Devil. You've come a long way."

"Thanks mate. You've got to be true to yourself, eh."

John could tell Blair wanted him to engage on the point of his true self. Blair obviously believed that the warlike creature he had seen on numerous occasions during their time in the drug world was who John really was. Whether Blair was right or not, John was not prepared to go there. He just sat quietly until Blair spoke again

"So, what are you going to do with all this money mate?"

"I haven't thought too much about it Blair. I just want to use it to live well and live free. I want to have money, so I don't have to spend my life chasing money."

"I get you mate, but that answer's no fun. Don't you want to buy a speedboat or get a mould of your nuts made in gold or something?"

John chuckled.

"I suppose if I was going to blow some of the money on a crazy luxury item, I'd probably buy a DeLorean."

"What, the car from Back to the Future?"

"Yep. Coolest car ever."

"You can't even bloody drive mate," Blair joked.

"I know, but you want me to be crazy with the money and that's what I'd do."

"Wouldn't you want like a Ferrari or some other modern sports car?"

"Nah mate, like I said, a DeLorean is the coolest car ever. Plus it was made in Belfast."

"No way! I thought DeLorean cars were made in America."

"Wash your mouth out Blair. No, they were made in Belfast. My granda actually used to work in the factory."

"Fucking hell, I never knew that. So the main reason you want one, apart from the fact that it's a cool car, is because it was made in Belfast?"

"Yep."

"Wasn't the Titanic made in Belfast?"

"Fuck off."

At this point, they both laughed.

"So, it looks like I'll have to take no for an answer?" Blair clarified.

"Sorry mate. But even though I can't get bloody, ask me for anything else. Any advice you need on strategy or a next move. Anything at all."

"Thanks mate. I'm gonna need all the help I can get. This is shaping up to be the biggest drug war in Australian history."

Chapter Eight

Blair made his way out through the white marble foyer of John's apartment building, filled with disappointment that - in his mind at least - his friend had let him down. He was now overcome with trepidation about what would come next in this quickly spiralling drug war.

It wasn't that he didn't understand John's reasons for being unwilling to get his hands dirty, he just thought John would have felt compelled to help him, regardless of what grounds there might be not to. After almost losing his life in Manchester helping John take down The Brotherhood, Blair felt John owed him a lot.

He didn't have time to reflect on this for long, as he walked through the main door of the apartment building to find a familiar face waiting for him on the front steps. It was Terence, one of his gang members.

Terence was a bit different from the other members of the gang. In many ways, he was the runt of the litter.

He was a lot smaller and less well built than the rest of them and his combat skills were nowhere near the standard of the other guys.

Blair had trained with him many times and tried to raise up his skill set, but it didn't come naturally to him at all. Blair always made a point of partnering him up for drug dealing with someone who could really handle themselves and looked it as well.

If Terence were to try dealing drugs in a club on his own, Blair felt sure he would get robbed and beaten within minutes. That said, Terence probably viewed himself as being as tough as the rest of them.

If anything, he talked tougher than anyone else in the gang, always threatening to beat the fuck out of people, or saying he was going to kill someone over the slightest thing. Of course, no one in the gang took this seriously, as he was no match for any of them.

To an extent, he was a kind of joke within the gang. He was all talk, no action - just a small man with a Napoleon complex.

Blair was never completely sure if Terence really thought of himself as tough, or if maybe he just thought that he was, in some way, convincing the others he was hard as nails with his behaviour. Thinking that if he threatened to beat the fuck out of someone and they let it go, he had proved himself on some level.

The only time he really showed any kind of toughness was when he had plenty of back up and could flaunt his sadistic streak.

If they had a rival drug dealer pinned down outside in the street, in a nightclub or bar, or snatched away to somewhere private and out of the way, Terence would always be the first one in line to pull out a knife and start cutting them.

He loved violence when there was no chance he could get hurt or that he would have his weakness exposed.

Terence had more than the usual amount of Aussie bravado, acting hard and talking tough all the time, even if he lacked the strength and courage to back it up. He took himself very seriously.

He liked to be called either Terry, El Tel or just Tel. A lot of the guys in the gang went along with this, but Blair made a point of always calling him Terence, just as John had done when he was in charge of the gang.

Neither John nor Blair were fans of people taking themselves too seriously. Pride comes before a fall, they both thought.

The only reason Terence had managed to survive in the gang this long was because of the extent to which he went out of his way to look after everyone in the group, help them out with things in their lives, offer advice, or just check that they were okay. He was seen as the nice guy of the bunch, the caring one. This overshadowed his weakness and absurd tough talking within the ranks of the gang.

Terence even had two young daughters, Hayley and Katlin.

He'd got a couple of different girls pregnant in his teenage years and somehow ended up with custody of the two children, although his father and his sister did most of the actual parenting. Nevertheless, he would always say that the two girls were his life and he even had each of their names tattooed on the inside of his wrists.

This caring persona meant that the guys in the gang were inclined to look out for him.

The inclination to look after him and cut him a lot of slack was helped further by the fact that he always had a bag of powder in his pocket for personal use and he was generous with it among the other gang members. Sometimes it was cocaine, but more often than not, it was crystal methamphetamine.

Crystal meth was a drug that the gang didn't sell, but Terence had a source for it. The novelty of a drug that the guys didn't have easy access to meant that it was always well received by them.

Blair was no different in this respect; he was always grateful for a little bump of crystal, to put an inch in his step. Blair had commented in the past that the likes of ambulance drivers and mountain rescue guys should carry a bag of crystal meth on them, as the immediate recuperative powers of the drug were second to no other substance, in his view.

He hadn't been expecting to meet Terence here and was not sure what he wanted, although he had his suspicions.

He'd felt compelled to give Terence a serious warning just the previous week over his relationship with an underage girl. This was the second time an episode like this had happened. There had now been two separate incidents that Blair was aware of, with two different girls, and Terence had been told after the first time never to do it again.

The first occasion had been only a few months previously. Terence had got a thirteen-year-old girl pregnant and Blair and the gang had to get involved to stop the family going to the police and take care of the costs and arrangements for the girl's abortion, as well as giving the girl and her family a substantial payoff. Money and the threat of violence had been used to smooth things over with the girl and her family.

Terence had pleaded ignorance over how young the girl was, claiming she had told him she was eighteen. She certainly looked older than thirteen when she was dressed up and wearing make up, heels etc, so Blair had believed him. Now that it had happened again, it seemed that maybe this claim of unawareness had been a lie and that Terence had, what they call in prison, 'short eyes'. Perhaps he was a little too keen on underage girls - a short man with short eyes.

Blair had come down on him like a ton of bricks and told him that if he ever saw this girl again, or if something like this ever happened again, he'd be out of the gang with a bullet.

Terence had seemed to take the warning on board and appeared to show remorse.

Blair reasoned that he was probably there waiting for him to try to worm his way back into his good graces.

He smiled up at Blair, as he made his way down the steps. Terence's single gold hoop earring glinted in the Sydney sun.

"G'day mate, how are you going?"

"Good thanks Terence. I wasn't expecting to see you here."

"Ah yeah, Nate said you'd be down here and I wanted to check you were okay. He said you came without back up."

"I'm fine mate, yeah. It's all good. Me and John together can handle anyone."

Blair got to the bottom of the steps and the two of them began walking side by side up the street.

"How is John?"

"He seems great mate. All loved up with his girl, looking good."

"Is he gonna help with the war?"

Blair noted that Terence was asking questions in a quick-fire style, but he put it down to a keenness to impress and make conversation.

"No mate, John is out. He'll help out with advice and other stuff, but he won't be getting his gun on."

"Fuck, that's a shame, especially after you went to Manchester to go to war for him."

Blair didn't react to this and just continued walking in silence.

"So, what's the plan now?"

"The plan now is that if Hatchet Willis and The Hatchet Mob want a war, then we take them to war; all the way."

Terence nodded and smiled, as if this was somehow what he wanted to hear.

They walked a little further up the street and Blair was really just caught up in his own racing thoughts, despite having company with him in the form of the diminutive Terence.

He was only half looking as a figure emerged from behind a large black van, parked at the edge of the curb, and stood there facing him and Terence. This snapped Blair out of his cloud of inner thoughts and back into his immediate reality.

The person facing them was the imposing and menacing Hatchet Willis.

"G'day guys. Nice day for it," said Willis.

Blair had no time to react or respond, as he received a hard and sharp blow to the back of the head, knocking him unconscious.

Chapter Nine

John's Sydney apartment had a modern, luxurious, spacious and airy feel. Everything was easily accessible from the central open plan living area, although there was a short, narrow hallway running off it to the bathroom, and the front door had kind of a semi-hallway, with a wall running for a short distance at either side of the doorway. One wall was at the edge of the kitchen area; the other wall turned the corner to the hallway leading to the bathroom.

The bedroom doors and the balcony door were accessible directly from the living room part of the main open plan area, although at different sides.

John closed the balcony door behind him with his left hand, as he returned to the balcony holding a freshly poured glass of his favourite Australian iced coffee milkshake in his right. Lisa had just made her way down the tight hallway to the bathroom, after their brief conversation.

The discussion had been short and cold, barely concealing the ashes of a past argument and some ongoing issues between them.

Lisa was adamant that under no circumstances should John go back into the drug world, not for any reason. They had locked horns over this in Hong Kong and again when they first got to Sydney.

John knew she was right in many ways, but he felt a huge sense of loyalty to Blair and a deep sense of obligation to help him in his hour of need, even if that meant holding guns in his hands again and making a limited return to Sydney's underworld. There was only so far he could push her on this, however, given what had happened to them both as a result of his criminal activities in the past.

The exchange between John and Lisa after Blair had left had been little more than a clarification that John had stuck to the agreed terms, following their previous conversations. Lisa wanted to be sure that he had not allowed himself to be talked into getting involved in the violence again.

John was frustrated and plagued by feelings of guilt as he sat by himself on the balcony, looking across Circular Quay at the Opera House. The sun reflected brightly off the surface of its roof, making it appear white from a distance, rather that the yellowy, grubby, off-white colour it actually was when you looked at the tile up close.

It had been brutally difficult for John to look Blair in the eye and refuse to help him, particularly after Blair had travelled right around the world to fight a war in Manchester alongside him that was really none of his affair.

John would love to have fully reciprocated, but had to merely offer advice as a kind of drug war consultant. Perhaps this could be a new career for him going forward, he laughingly thought to himself.

If John was completely honest with himself, coupled with the overwhelming sense of shame over the issue was also something of a feeling of relief. After everything that had happened over the previous couple of years, in Manchester and in Sydney, John really did want to be out of that life. The events had traumatised and changed him.

The days of him enjoying violence, to some extent, and having a taste for it had long since passed. The extremes of bloodshed and brutality he had seen and been part of since he'd first become involved with The Brotherhood had sickened him of this.

If anything, he had come to hate violence. Not that he had stopped his martial training, but now he was doing it out of a pure appreciation of the martial arts, rather than as preparation for inevitable necessary conflict.

The deaths haunted him, especially those of the three individuals who'd been best friends of his. Two of them had died his best friends; one had betrayed him and become an enemy before his demise.

What they all had in common was that John blamed himself for their deaths.

Peter had sold him out to The Brotherhood; there was no getting away from that. John had killed him only a matter of hours after finding this out, albeit in self-defence.

Having had a chance to reflect on it, since that fateful night of New Year's Eve 2002, John had been forced to admit to himself that some of Peter's grievances, which had set him on the path to double-crossing John, had been valid to some degree; not that this was an excuse for his monumental treachery. John still felt a certain amount of remorse for putting that bullet in his brain though.

Michael had lied to him, but never really double-crossed him; although by the rules of The Brotherhood, which John had subscribed to at the time, he had betrayed them all. And while John had not put any bullets in him, he'd been part of the death squad that took his life.

John had failed to help him that night. He had been an observer as Michael had been physically, mentally and emotionally tortured, and his mother raped, thinking of intervening, but never doing so. Ultimately, he had even played an active role in burying him alive. John had recurring nightmares about the various horrifying and disgusting aspects of what happened that night.

In many ways, Alan was the worst of the deaths of his friends and the one John felt the most self-condemnation about. He'd been a lifelong friend of his, since childhood in Belfast, and had got involved in John's spree of violent revenge in Manchester purely out of loyalty. Unlike Blair, he had not been promised any money or material gain if the mission was successful and had never been part of the drug dealing underworld.

Although John had played no active part in Alan being brutally cut to pieces, while he was still alive, John felt strongly that it was his fault. Plus he felt hugely conscience-stricken that his family were still in the dark as to what had happened to him; Alan was just another missing person who could not be found.

Even though he was regretful about it now, John reasoned that Lisa had ultimately done him a favour by putting her foot down over the drug war. At heart, John didn't want any more blood on his hands. He didn't know how much more violence and death he could take on his conscience.

It was time to look forward and move on. John felt like he had been preparing for life since grammar school and never really started living. Even now, as he sat there in his mid-twenties, he still looked at life as if he was waiting to start, to some extent.

Going through the traditional education route of grammar school followed by university had a tendency to grind that outlook into your brain; the idea that everything you were doing was a kind of preparation for a life you had yet to start living.

John had carried that mentality into his dead-end, post-university jobs, his round the world travel, and even his segue into the world of drug dealing.

It was time for him to embrace his life with Lisa moving forward. He needed to leave the violence in the past.

Lisa had come out of the bathroom now and was back in the main living area of the apartment, pottering around the kitchen part, when the buzzer sounded.

John remained sitting on the balcony, assuming that Blair had popped back, having forgotten something, and that Lisa would let him in. Lisa also presumed it was a forgetful Blair making a return and buzzed open the main door of the building, without a second thought. She then lingered near the apartment door, ready to open it when the knock came.

John braced himself for more awkwardness and embarrassment in dealing with Blair again, having just let him down.

Then, at the last second, a thought occurred to him. What if they were both wrong and it wasn't Blair? Who might Lisa have just buzzed into the building and who was she about to open the apartment door to?

The door of the apartment had several deadbolt locks on it, spread out evenly down the length of the strong, heavy door. John had fitted them for extra safety and security, during the height of his drug dealing days in Sydney.

However, none of these had been re-locked after Blair had left and the only lock holding the door shut was the security lock, which enabled the person inside to open the door slightly, while still having an element of protection. It was one of the solid metal swing bar ones, rather than one of those with a metal chain.

John opened up the balcony door to re-enter the apartment, just as the knock came to the door. Lisa was beginning to take off the swing bar lock, in order to pull the door fully open, when John shouted abruptly at her and stopped her in her tracks.

"Stop! Don't open it!"

Lisa spun round bewildered, but did stop opening the door. John dashed across the main apartment area and slammed the security lock back in place, before taking a look through the peephole. It was not Blair.

Standing at the door was a relatively rough looking guy, approximately in his mid-twenties, with his hair cut in a kind of tame mohican, with the sides of his black hair not fully shaved and the top dyed blonde. He was looking sheepish and eager for the door to be opened; he had obviously heard the tampering with the swing bar lock going on inside.

John started closing the deadbolts on the door as he turned to Lisa with his finger over his mouth, indicating that she should be quiet. He then began talking to the guy through the door, to stall him, as he got all the deadbolts locked.

"Hey mate, can I help you?"

"Ah yeah mate, I just need to talk to you about your plumbing," came the reply through the door.

"Oh yeah, what's wrong?"

"There's a bit of a leak coming down mate. If you open the door, I just need to check your bathroom."

"Can you come back another time mate?" asked John, as he got the bottom deadbolt locked and stood back up to look out through the peephole again.

"I really need to get in now mate."

John didn't reply this time and just continued watching through the peephole.

"Hello. Can I get in mate?" came the next request from this stranger with the mohican, but again John gave no reply.

John could sense Lisa getting nervous and restless behind him, but he remained focussed on staring through the peephole. He didn't have to wait long before he got a full reveal of what was going on.

An arm came into view and tapped the alleged plumber on the shoulder, as if to tap him out of his failed attempt to get into the apartment. As the rest of the person attached to this arm became visible, John was shocked and horrified, as he realised the seriousness of their predicament.

The face of the individual was all too familiar, especially given that John had made his mark on it with a horrific scar; it was Hatchet Willis.

Willis gave a signal to the rest of his men, who had been hiding out of sight of the peephole. Suddenly, the view from John's peephole became filled with members of The Hatchet Mob.

There were a lot of them. John and Lisa were in grave and immediate danger.

Chapter Ten

All the members of The Hatchet Mob who were there were wearing trench coats, apart from the one with the mohican who had knocked the door. This was not surprising, as the trench coat was their signature garment.

As John looked on through the peephole, they began pulling out weapons that had been concealed beneath their trench coats: mostly hatchets, axes and machetes, although one of them produced a full-length double barrel shotgun.

The Hatchet Mob knew that they had been rumbled and had dispensed with trickery and subterfuge.

They were about to attempt to storm the place. All the players in the game now knew what was happening, apart from an increasingly panicked Lisa.

John spun around to face her and pulled her close to him, so he could whisper in her ear.

"We're in trouble. We're under attack. I need you to go to the bathroom for me and get in the bath."

"What? But - "

John held his finger to her mouth, to indicate that she needed to whisper in the same way he had. Just at this moment, the familiar voice of Hatchet Willis came booming through the door.

"G'day Johnny Boy, you fuckin' cunt! You might as well let us in, or we're gonna have to huff and puff!"

"I'm just getting the keys mate," John shouted back. "I can't wait to see that lovely scar on your face up close."

John did not need a key to open the door from the inside, nor did he especially want to closely inspect the facial scar he'd given Hatchet Willis. All he was trying to do at this point was stall The Hatchet Mob, before they would inevitably force their way in.

His priority now was to try to get Lisa in as safe a position as he could and get himself as prepared as he could be, before they came through the door.

"Who is it John? What's going on?" asked Lisa, at the appropriate volume, but obviously terrified.

"It's The Hatchet Mob. We're in trouble. You need to do what I say and go to the bathroom. Get in the bath and I'll be in there in a minute," John hurriedly whispered in response.

This time he got through to Lisa and she nodded, moving away from the doorway, turning the corner and hurrying down the narrow hallway to the bathroom.

She wasn't sure why she was supposed to get in the bath, but she got in anyway, lying down in the foetal position.

John realised he had very little time left, as the loud bangs of someone slamming their body against the door began.

"Open the fuckin' door, you fuckin' fairy!" Hatchet Willis called through the door, as the relentless banging continued.

John knew they had hatchets, axes and a double barrel shotgun. The deadbolts would slow them down and there was no way they were kicking this door down, but with all those tools at their disposal, there was no doubt that they would be getting in.

Before leaving Sydney, after the attack by The Brotherhood, John had cleared out all remaining guns and weapons from the apartment. He now deeply regretted doing this, but there was no time to reflect on what he could have done differently. The past is history. There was only time for quick thinking and swift action.

John ran into the kitchen part of the open plan living space, just around the corner from the semi-hallway area at the doorway. He had a wooden block that held four kitchen knives, which he had sharpened to an incredibly high degree. They were so razor-sharp that Lisa refused to use them, fearing that she might lose a finger.

These extra sharp knives were about to come in handy, as they were the closest things to weapons that he had at his disposal.

He'd counted at least six members of The Hatchet Mob, when he was looking through the peephole. Considering how well armed they were, as well as the fact that they had him hugely outnumbered, John knew it was going to take everything he had to save Lisa and get them out of the apartment alive. One wrong judgement, one wrong move, going right when he should go left, and they were both dead.

John was in survival mode now though, and all thoughts of the odds against him or the possible repercussions of coming off worst in this forthcoming battle had no place in his mind.

He knew he had to give himself to the fight, forget any concerns about his personal welfare or any fear and use all his training and combat experience to get them out of this.

As the body slams against the door turned into the sharp chops of an axe being crashed into it, John was at the corner at the end of the semi-hallway area around the doorway, where it turned into the tight hallway to the bathroom. This would be the point he would try not to let the intruders pass, having already accepted that they would be coming through the door.

Standing just around the corner from where they would be able to see when they entered, John had three of the carving knives from the wooden block in his left hand, having left the block and the smallest one of the knives in the kitchen area.

He took the largest one of them in his right hand and stabbed it into the wall, at around the height of the top of his chest, so that it was sticking out with the blade facing sideways away from him, in the direction that any intruder would be trying to come.

He then took a second knife in his right hand and chopped it into the corner of the wall, at around the level of his shin, so that the tip of it was peeking around the corner into the semi-hallway area leading to the doorway.

The third one he tucked into the back of the cargo shorts he was wearing, as he made his way along the hallway to the bathroom.

As he walked, he could hear the chopping at the door getting louder and more frenzied and intense. It seemed likely that two members of The Hatchet Mob were now trying to smash their way in at the same time. John did not have long.

He burst into the bathroom to find Lisa lying in the bath in the foetal position.

"Good, that's perfect baby!" he declared, as he hurriedly grabbed all of the towels from the raised metal towel rack against the wall and threw them into the bath at her feet.

"Give me your hand," he said, as he made his way to the far end of the bath, where her head was, and extended his right hand down to her.

She was visibly shaken, but she followed his instruction and held out her hand. John firmly pulled her up to her feet, so that she was standing up in the bath, and then guided her out on to the bathroom floor.

The banging of the axes hacking into the door was audible down the hallway into the bathroom, which was not helping to calm Lisa down.

"Okay, that was perfect; the way you were lying. I need you to lock the bathroom door behind me, get back in the bath, exactly like you were before, and pull all those towels over you like blankets, until you're completely covered. Do you understand?"

Lisa just nodded in response. John had his hands on her shoulders and he could feel her shaking.

"It's going to be okay Lisa. I promise it will be okay. I love you."

Before Lisa had time to respond, John dashed back out of the bathroom and made his way back along the narrow hallway, only stopping for a second to turn his head and check that Lisa had locked the bathroom door behind him.

He ran past the two knives he had stuck in the wall and across to the other side of the doorway hall area, into the kitchen part of the main living space. He made it across just as the first shotgun blast tore through the wooden door at the point where one of the deadbolts was.

They had obviously realised it was taking too long to get in using the axes, because of how strong and well secured the door was, and opted instead to blow the locks off with the shotgun.

John pulled the knife out from the back of his cargo shorts and crouched down at the edge of the kitchen area, just round the corner from the door that was being blown apart by shotgun pellets. Another shot blew off another chunk of the door and another deadbolt.

They would need to reload and use another one or two more shotgun shells to get through the door. Then they would pour in, mob-handed and armed to the teeth.

All thoughts of putting violence behind him, or of anything other than this deadly moment, went out of his head. It would take everything he'd learned and everything he had within him to stay alive and protect Lisa now.

Chapter Eleven

It took four blasts from the shotgun to destroy the deadbolt locks and most of the door, which had already been damaged by the axes. John remained crouching, at the ready, with his razor-sharp carving knife in hand, just around the corner from where they would enter.

The member of The Hatchet Mob with the double barrel shotgun reloaded it and entered through the doorway first, with the firearm extended and ready to fire. Within a couple of seconds, he set his sights on his selected target. He could see the tip of a knife peeking around the side of a wall and closed in on it, all set to point the gun at the person he imagined was holding it.

This was just what John had wanted and he watched from his vantage point, at the other side of the semi-hallway area, as the long barrel of the shotgun came into his view.

The time was at hand to act with violent decisiveness and with the deadly intent that could save his girlfriend's life and perhaps his own.

When the shotgun-wielding gang member moved outwards from the wall, into the middle of the semi-hallway area, to better and more safely aim his gun at his intended low target, John sprang into action. The gang member was left handed and was holding the shotgun with the index finger of his left hand on the trigger, which actually helped John in his plan to subdue and disarm this first of the many attackers.

As he got to the correct firing angle, he could see that what he thought was John, kneeling down and holding a knife, was in fact just a knife wedged into the wall. John pounced on him from behind and, with speed and accuracy, sliced down on his trigger finger with the exceptionally sharp carving knife, chopping it off with one swift and forceful motion.

The injured Hatchet Mob member screamed out and his fellow gang members began streaming through the door. John tore the shotgun out of his grip, with his left hand, and threw it to the ground at the beginning of the narrow hallway to the bathroom. This was the hallway he could not allow The Hatchet Mob to get through.

With his forearm, John thrust the gang member - who was now missing a finger and shrieking with pain - forwards using all his body weight and all the force and momentum he could muster.

The gang member wasn't fighting back much, due to the shock and pain of having his finger cut off. He continued wailing, as John used his left hand to grab the back of his hair, at the last second, and pull his head back, so that his throat was fully exposed. He slammed his throat, as hard as he could, into the razor sharp blade of the large knife facing them, which he had stuck in the wall at the perfect height.

The knife cut deep into his throat, leaving him attached to the blade, as he almost hung from it. Even if he were able to extricate himself from this bloody predicament, he would effectively kill himself, as now the only thing stopping him from bleeding to death in seconds was the blade of the knife stuck halfway through his neck.

John spun around just in time to see the next wave of The Hatchet Mob reaching him. The first one to get to him had an axe, while the two just behind him - closing in side by side - were wielding hatchets.

As the axe came chopping down at him, aimed for the centre of his head, John just managed to slip it, moving to his left, like a boxer slipping a savage metal punch. He then came swinging up and forwards with the carving knife in his right hand, the blade running along his forearm, with the sharpened edge facing outwards at his human target.

He jumped forcefully forwards, throwing his weight into the lethal knife blow, which cut deeply and expeditiously through the side of this attacker's neck, like a warm knife cutting through soft butter.

As the knife slid out and forwards from this gang member's neck and John's momentum took him forward towards the next two members of The Hatchet Mob, he flicked part of the massive spurt of blood from the first Hatchet Mob member's neck into the eyes of the attacker closing in to his left.

He then spun the knife skilfully around in his hand, so that the heavily bloodied sharp edge of it was now facing the opponent closing in to his right, and punched the blunt side of the knife blade with the bottom of his left fist, splashing blood into the eyes of this hatchet ready member of The Hatchet Mob, just as he swung his hatchet downwards at John. He ducked sideways and down to his left, dropping the knife from his right to his left hand as he did so, and just avoiding the impending hatchet blow.

Holding the blade so that it was pointing downwards with the sharp edge facing out, he moved up and forwards, slicing the knife through the trousers of the attacker to his left at the inner thigh, cutting deep into the artery. Then he continued moving upwards with the blade, above the deep cut he had just created, as blood sprayed out intensely from the open wound.

He brought the point of the knife level with the neck of his other temporarily blinded attacker and powerfully thrust the blade right through it. He left the knife skewered through this gang member's neck, before tipping his head and upper body backwards to avoid an incoming blow from a machete, as the onslaught from The Hatchet Mob continued.

John turned around and bolted for the start of the hallway to the bathroom, ducking down to grab the double barrel shotgun when he reached it and popping up with it pointed at the head of the gang member with the mohican, who had almost closed in on him, axe at the ready.

"Don't fucking move you cunt! That goes for the rest of you fuckers too!" he shouted, his finger on the trigger of the shotgun.

The mohican haired member of The Hatchet Mob didn't come any closer, but he didn't retreat either. The rest of them stopped in their tracks.

"Put the fucking weapons down, before I put holes in you!"

"You've only got two bullets mate," pointed out Hatchet Willis.

Now that John had a clear view of them all, he could see that Willis did indeed have a point.

There was the gang member with the mohican haircut, who was holding an axe, another gang member, who was holding a machete, Hatchet Willis, who was holding a hatchet, and his lieutenant Fletcher - who John recognised from their previous violent encounter at the Sydney nightclub Spice - who was also armed with a hatchet.

He had given both Hatchet Willis and Fletcher a limp, during their last fight in the toilets of Spice, as well as giving Willis the severe looking scar on the side of his face.

After this incident, both Hatchet Willis and Fletcher had been very eager to carve him up and kill him as brutally as they could. In this moment though, they had to accept that John had a fully loaded double barrel shotgun pointed at them. At the same time, John had to take on board Hatchet Willis' point that there were four members of The Hatchet Mob facing off against him and he only had two bullets.

They had given him the well-earned underworld respect he deserved and come after him with eight heavily armed men, but three of them were now bleeding out in the doorway hall area of his apartment. Another of them was still impaled on the carving knife stuck in the wall, just to John's left.

John could see this guy was still alive, after briefly looking at him in his peripheral vision, but he kept his eyes chiefly focussed on the four members of The Hatchet Mob stood in front of him, as the one skewered by the throat to his left could not pose him any threat, or even move without killing himself.

"I see. I've got two bullets and there are four of you ready for action; is that what you're thinking Scarface? Well, that means only two of you will definitely die, if you don't put the weapons down. Which two of you fannies fancy it?"

John could see the cogs turning in their heads, as they mulled over their options and considered what John had said.

"If you use those two shells, you really think you could take the other two of us before we chop you up?" asked Hatchet Willis.

"I think if I kill two of you with this shotgun, I could pull my dick out and beat the fuck out of the other two with it," was John's fearless reply.

Hatchet Willis sniggered. He admired John's courage and swagger under fire, even if he did hate him with a vengeance and want to tear him to pieces.

John kept his shotgun trained on the gang member with the mohican haircut right in front of him, although he lowered it slightly, so that it was pointing at his torso rather than his head.

Still this gang member was holding the axe and still the other three had not dropped their weapons. If anything, the member of The Hatchet Mob with the mohican and the axe seemed to be closer to swinging it at John than he did to dropping it.

John knew if he let the standoff continue much longer, they were likely to get less nervous and make a run at him. He was still the only thing between them and Lisa and there was no way he could allow them to get past him, even if it cost him his life. He had to do something now, to get them to lower their weapons and get them out of the apartment.

"Okay ladies, you've got five seconds to put your weapons down, or I will drop two of you, starting with Green Day here."

"You can't win mate," replied Willis.

"Five."

"You die today, cunt!" added Fletcher.

"Four."

They all grew increasingly twitchy, as they realised John was going through with the five second countdown.

"Three."

The gang member with the mohican, who John had referred to as Green Day, was tightening his grip on the axe in his hand.

"Two."

Time was running out and they did not seem to be lowering their weapons. John had hoped they wouldn't call his bluff and that this tactic would have been enough to bring about a controlled surrender and a retreat.

It seemed now that it would not be sufficient and they were going to test his resolve and play the odds, to make sure he didn't get out of this alive.

"One."

Chapter Twelve

The Hatchet Mob was infamous across Australia and their leader, Hatchet Willis, was a kind of household name. He was the sort of celebrity criminal who would bring a wry smile to the faces of a lot of people, like Ned Kelly had before him, or someone like Al Capone had in the United States.

The Hatchet Mob had been on the warpath ever since Hatchet Willis and Fletcher had recovered from the injuries inflicted on them by John Kennedy.

All that pain, all that time, all that recovery, all that agonising physiotherapy had just made them more angry and more determined.

They were utterly resolute that they were going to reclaim their territory and claim as much additional turf as they could. More than this, they were totally resolved to take away territory from what had been John's gang - but was now Blair's - and inflict maximum hurt on all of its members, as well as former leader John.

John had been earmarked for a painful, slow death for a long time. Now he stood face to face with a Hatchet Mob death squad, counting down to the breakpoint of an armed standoff.

He had a double barrel shotgun, which he had taken from one of their gang members, in his hands, trained at the torso of the member of The Hatchet Mob with the distinctive mohican haircut, who'd tried to trick his way into John's apartment masquerading as a plumber. Why they had selected one of their gang members with such an unusual hairstyle to try to play the role of an ordinary, everyday plumber, John did not know.

John would probably have worked out that it was a trick anyway, regardless of who Hatchet Willis had chosen for the job. Anyone who wasn't Blair was going to have to work very hard, and answer a lot of questions, to get through the door to his apartment in that moment.

As he reached the number one in his countdown from five, none of The Hatchet Mob members before him had dropped their weapons, nor did it seem likely they would. If anything, they seemed like they were calling John's bluff and perhaps preparing to charge on him. John could not afford to be seen to be bluffing.

The gang member with the mohican had been growing increasing twitchy. As the countdown had progressed he'd seemed to tighten his grip on the axe in his hand, as if he was preparing to strike a blow on John with it.

This twitchiness, added to the fact that the shotgun was trained so closely on him and that John knew he had no choice but to act, made up his mind for him.

Immediately that the countdown ended, John pulled the trigger on the shotgun, blowing a large hole right through the middle of the gang member with the mohican. A look of shock was frozen on his face as he launched backwards and downwards through the air, landing in a bloody mess at the feet of Hatchet Willis, Fletcher and the other member of The Hatchet Mob who was still unharmed.

They were all sprayed with blood from their now deceased fellow gang member and were just stood there, frozen in their tracks. They still had not put down their weapons, however.

John trained the shotgun on the torso of Hatchet Willis himself, thinking that this would get him the most value from his one remaining shotgun shell.

"You're next Willis, you fuckin' ball bag!" he announced to his new target.

Hatchet Willis paused for a second to process this, then wiped the blood from his face with his left hand and dropped the hatchet he was holding from his right.

"Put 'em down boys," was his instruction to the other two.

They did as he instructed, although it was clear to John from the look on Fletcher's face that he didn't entirely agree with his boss's decision.

Fletcher didn't argue the point though; very few people were foolish enough to argue any point with Hatchet Willis.

"What now Johnno? You just gonna point that gun at me all day?"

"Now you and your little gal pals get the fuck out of my apartment, before I blow a hole in you."

"And what about my two mates here? You think you can kill me and they'll just fuck off and leave you and your bitch alone?"

"That won't be your problem mate. The dead don't need to worry about the living; that'll be between me and The Cheeky Girls here."

Hatchet Willis looked into his eyes and knew he wasn't bluffing.

He was not afraid, but he was determined that, out of the two of them, John would be the one to die and not him. And he wanted to make sure that he made him, Blair and everyone in their gang suffer as much as possible.

It went against his pride and his hard as nails mentality, but he knew they would have to bow out this time.

"We'll see you soon Johnny Boy."

"Shut up and fuck off, you fucking cock."

Hatchet Willis gave the nod to Fletcher and the other gang member, indicating that they were leaving. Again the other two followed Willis' instruction and once again Fletcher seemed the most reluctant to obey.

As the three of them edged towards the front door of the apartment, they kept their eyes fixed on John and he kept the shotgun fixed on Hatchet Willis. With each step they took backwards, he took one forwards, until he was standing at the front door.

He stood there in the doorway, pointing the gun out into the main hallway of his floor of the apartment building, while the three Hatchet Mob members were standing there waiting for the lift.

"You don't have long to live mate. Enjoy it while it lasts," were Hatchet Willis' parting words to John, as he followed Fletcher and the other gang member into the elevator and the elevator door closed behind them.

Once John was sure they were safely in the lift and that it was on its way down, John lowered the shotgun that had helped save his life and the life of his girlfriend. Almost as soon as he did so, he began to hear the sound of distant police sirens.

As he stepped back into the apartment filled with dead bodies, shotgun held in his hands, he himself was covered in their blood. The walls and floor of the apartment were also covered in blood and a Hatchet Mob member was still hanging by the throat from the knife stuck in his wall, waiting to die.

John now had a new problem.

Even though everything he'd done had been in self-defence, he felt that he would have a tough time explaining this to the police. The approaching sirens meant trouble and probably prison.

They had to get out of there fast.

Chapter Thirteen

John had fought bravely and intelligently to save his life and the life of his girlfriend. He was now in the middle of a blood-spattered mess that was soon to become a police crime scene and Lisa was still locked in the bathroom, lying down in the bath, covered in towels.

The sirens from the cop cars were getting louder, although John reckoned they were still far enough away that he and Lisa had perhaps just enough time to get out and get away, before law enforcement locked the place down.

His body was still flooded with adrenaline and he needed to stay in fifth gear and use his heightened state to get them out and clear.

He wiped the shotgun with his t-shirt, around the trigger and the places where he'd been holding it, and dropped it in the middle of the bloody hall area, just inside the doorway of his apartment.

He then took off his t-shirt and knelt down beside the gang member lying on the ground with the knife stuck through his neck - who was almost dead, but not quite - and wiped the handle of the knife with the cotton garment in his hand, leaving the knife in position, stuck in his victim.

John did the same with the handles of the other two knives stuck in the wall, again leaving the knife that was wedged halfway through a gang member's neck in place, before running into the kitchen area of the main living space.

He opened up the kitchen bin, dropped his t-shirt into it, and began frantically stripping and dropping the rest of his bloodied items of clothing into the tall, metal rubbish receptacle, including his blood-soaked trainers.

Once he was stripped down to his underwear, he turned on both taps at the kitchen sink, so that the water was blasting powerfully out and spraying up at him from the metal basin. He sloshed water all over himself and used squirts of washing up liquid to get as much blood off him as he could in a few seconds.

He then picked up a tea towel and gave himself a quick once-over with it, to get him dry enough to proceed, and threw the now blood-stained tea towel into the same tall metal kitchen bin.

After this quick strip and clean up, he took the lid off the kitchen bin and pulled out the black rubbish bag that lined it.

There were only a couple of bits of rubbish in the bag, along with the bloodied clothes and tea towel John had just thrown into it.

He flung open one of the kitchen drawers and hastily grabbed a bottle of lighter fluid and his silver Zippo lighter, which was engraved with the words, 'THE DOORS Light Your Fire'.

John tied the black rubbish bag closed and threw it across the semi-hallway area at the front door and out through the doorway itself, so that it landed in the main hallway of his floor of the apartment building, beside the elevators.

He then made his way across the open plan living area to the door of the main bedroom, bringing the lighter fluid and the Zippo lighter with him.

He charged into the bedroom, flung open the wardrobe and grabbed the first t-shirt, jeans and boots that came to hand and put them on as quickly as he could. He shoved the lighter fluid and the lighter into the pocket of his jeans.

Once he was dressed in the clean clothes and showing no signs of blood, he darted out of the bedroom and along the narrow hallway to the bathroom.

He knocked the door hard and shouted through it to Lisa.

"Open the door baby, it's all clear! We need to hurry!"

He then banged the door again and could hear Lisa stirring from her hiding place in the bath and making her way to the door.

As she opened it, John pushed her back inside and closed the bathroom door behind them.

"Okay baby, we're nearly out of this," he said, taking a gentle hold of her by the shoulders. "What I need you to do for me now is close your eyes and don't open them till we're in the lift. I'm going to guide you."

"But why John? What has happened? Is everything okay now?"

"Everything's fine Lisa, but we need to go. We really have to get out of here and I need you trust me and keep your eyes closed. I'll explain everything later, but right now you definitely don't want to see what's out there. Once you see it, you won't be able to unsee it. Okay?"

"Okay," Lisa agreed, closing her eyes and bracing herself for this next ordeal.

John opened the bathroom door and moved around behind Lisa, placing his hands on the tops of her shoulders and firmly pushing her out in the direction of the hallway, although not so firmly that she might fall or stumble too far ahead and end up getting blood on her.

As they made their way along the tight hallway, towards the central living area of the apartment, Lisa was true to her word and kept her eyes firmly shut. She believed John when he told her she really didn't want to see what was out there and she wasn't going to let curiosity get the better of her.

She could hear the police sirens as they got louder and also the gasping, gargling sounds that came from the nearby member of The Hatchet Mob.

He was still hanging by the throat from the carving knife that was stuck in the wall at the end of this hallway.

When the pair got to the end of the hallway where this gang member was dangling, John carefully guided Lisa wide of him and the pool of blood around him.

Once they were past this red puddle, John turned Lisa ninety degrees to the left and aimed her between the other bodies and blood pools in the area.

Just before he pushed her forward, he took his left hand off her left shoulder and reached it back and sideways, taking hold of the collar of the dying gang member stuck on the knife blade. As he began pushing Lisa forwards with his right hand, he yanked the collar of this unfortunate member of The Hatchet Mob backwards and to the left, so that as he spun out and away from the blade that was holding the wound closed, the blood would spray out into the main living space and away from him and Lisa.

John didn't even look behind him, as the flailing gang member squirted a fountain of blood into the living room area, while he choked and spluttered his final breaths.

Lisa noticed the noise, but she realised that this was not the time to ask John about what was happening. She knew it was bad, but she also noticed that the police sirens were getting louder and nearer.

The cops were coming for them, as they made their way out of the blood-soaked apartment and into the main hallway area of this floor of the apartment building.

John positioned Lisa facing the elevator door, pressed the button to call it and picked up the black rubbish bag full of bloody evidence. The following seconds, waiting for the lift to come and watching the numbers above it light up, felt like an eternity.

John did his best to remain calm though and the moment the doors opened to reveal an empty lift, he pushed Lisa firmly inside, got in himself, holding the black trash bag in his hand, and pressed the button to take them down to the basement with the index finger of his other hand.

He then spun around to watch the LED display indicate the floor numbers as they passed them, hoping that the elevator would not stop until they hit the basement floor.

"Is it safe to open my eyes now?" asked Lisa.

She was virtually positive that it was, but wanted to be absolutely sure.

"Yes baby," answered John, as he anxiously watched the floor numbers tick down on the elevator display.

Just as they got past the floor of the lobby, the light lit up, indicating that the lift had been called to this floor and would make its way back up after they got out.

Judging by the timing and the little bits of bustling noise they could make out as they passed this floor, it was the police.

John now hoped that the cops would be more focussed on getting up to the crime scene than they would be on wondering if the people in the lift they had just missed had anything to do with the noisy and violent disturbance.

As the doors opened to the basement floor, they were both relieved to get out and see that the basement was clear of people. It was mainly used for underground parking for residents, although it also had a communal rubbish section filled with large dumpsters.

While the ramp up to the street, for cars driving out of the parking spaces, led right up to the front door part of the apartment building, there was a metal double door at the far side of the garbage part, which led out to the side street around the sloping corner from the main entrance.

John was gambling that the police would not have had time to secure the perimeter of the building yet and that this would be their best route to freedom.

"Come on," said John, taking Lisa by the hand and hurrying them to the rubbish section, carrying the black trash bag in his other hand.

John stopped beside the first metal dumpster in the garbage area, let go of Lisa's hand, opened up the green plastic lid and threw in the black rubbish bag.

He then took out the bottle of lighter fluid and the Zippo lighter, squirted the full contents of the lighter fluid bottle over the trash in the dumpster, dropped it in, flicked open the 'THE DOORS Light Your Fire' lighter, lit it and threw it into the dumpster, causing the contents to ignite into a ball of flames.

John took Lisa's hand again and they charged past the smelly, mostly filled dumpsters and got to the slightly rusted metal double door. There was no way to see what was on the other side.

"When we get out, we walk casually away from the building and don't look back. As soon as we're in the street, we've had nothing to do with this building. Yeah?"

"What if the police are out there?" asked Lisa.

John smiled.

"Then we're fucked. Are you ready?"

"Let's go."

John slid open the bolt holding the metal doors closed, looked at Lisa, nodded to indicate it was time to go and then pushed one of the doors open.

Chapter Fourteen

Blair had been conscious for a while now and had been struggling in the darkness of the grubby car boot. He'd been transferred from the back of the large black van into this car boot while he was still knocked out. His mouth, ankles and wrists were bound with elephant tape, so his attempts at attracting attention and trying to escape had been somewhat limited.

He estimated that the car had been stationary for at least an hour now and he was becoming resigned to the idea that when the boot opened, his fate would be in the hands of his enemies in the drug war - The Hatchet Mob.

He held little hope of walking away from this encounter alive. Blair was a tough and brave guy, but as he lay there in the trunk of this old car, waiting to be dealt with by The Hatchet Mob, he was terrified. He didn't want to die and he most certainly didn't want to die badly - as would be the most likely outcome.

As worried as he was for himself and his own fate, if anything, he was even more concerned about Terence, John and Lisa.

Terence had been with him when The Hatchet Mob struck, and he had just left John and Lisa in John's apartment before they'd grabbed him. Blair felt sure that the three of them had been on Hatchet Willis' hit list as well.

Was this the day that The Hatchet Mob would kill everyone?

Was this their Day of the Long Knives; or Day of the Long Hatchets?

Blair considered John to be one of his best friends, but even though they were close, had spent loads of time together, trained together, sold drugs together, and fought together, Blair was still a little bit in awe of him. Even after all the martial arts training and all the combat experience he'd had, not to mention target practice, he knew he could never get near the level John was at.

In a way, he thought of John as being invincible. He reasoned that if anyone could survive a surprise attack from The Hatchet Mob, it was John - especially when fighting and surviving would also mean protecting Lisa.

Terence, on the other hand, was nothing. When it came to combat and protecting himself, he was small, weak and under-trained.

He talked like he was the hardest man in Blair's gang and carried himself with the cocky swagger of someone who could handle anything, but this was all a front that wasn't fooling anyone who actually knew him.

Blair would have considered Terence pathetic and to be pitied, if he didn't like him so much and believe him to be the thoughtful, good guy of his gang; Mr. Caring. Terence was the runt of the litter and a bit of a joke, unlike the rest of the gang members, who could handle themselves extremely well.

That said, all of Blair's training hadn't really helped him in this situation, when Hatchet Willis popped out in front of him and someone whacked him on the back of the head, knocking him out. Perhaps Terence had been more fortunate and managed to strike a lucky blow or run away.

What was different about Terence compared to the rest of the gang - apart from his general weakness and the fact that he was all mouth and no trousers - was the fact that he had children. He was the father of two little girls and the idea of them being left without their dad, because of a conflict involving his gang, broke Blair's heart.

Granted, the two children were effectively being raised by Terence's father and his sister. Terence wasn't exactly a great parent, given that he was a criminal and a heavy drug user. He even kept and used drugs in the house where his daughters slept.

Still, the thought of this weighed heavily on Blair's conscience.

Blair could hear chatter and the clinking of keys and he braced himself for what was to come. The key turned in the lock of the boot and it opened up to reveal a smiling Hatchet Willis and Fletcher looking down on him.

"G'day mate. Sorry to keep you waiting," said Willis.

The pair of them wrenched the taped up Blair out of the trunk.

Willis took his feet and Fletcher took his upper body and as soon as they got him over the edge of the car boot, they dropped him on the concrete floor. Blair slammed down hard on to the ground and the harsh fluorescent strip lighting above him burned down into his eyes, which had become used to the darkness of his car boot prison.

"Welcome to hell, you little cunt," Fletcher announced with venom.

He and Hatchet Willis then began stomping on Blair, each of them using their good leg, having both been hobbled in the other leg by John with a butterfly knife. Blair did what little he could to cover up and protect himself, but he had to take the beating.

The assault went on for a while, before Hatchet Willis called a halt to it.

"That'll do. We want him to be awake for the best bit," he said.

Both Hatchet Willis and Fletcher then leaned down and stuck their hands under Blair's arms, trailing him around to the side of the car.

It was an old black Holden, from the nineteen-seventies, that had obviously either been well looked after or lovingly restored. They dropped Blair at the driver's side door and he rolled on to his back, giving him a chance to better take in his surroundings.

He was in a dingy, garage-style lock-up, with tools and engine parts lying around and grease spots on the floor. There were no windows and the breeze block and concrete interior was only illuminated by the fluorescent strip lighting above.

Fletcher pulled out a .38 revolver and pointed it at Blair's head, while Hatchet Willis reached down and pulled the piece of elephant tape from his mouth.

"Fuck you, you fuckin' cunts!" Blair shouted, as soon as his mouth was free.

Fletcher stomped down hard on his right kneecap as punishment and Blair did his best to stifle a scream of pain.

"Behave yourself, you little fucker," Fletcher advised.

"That's right, behave yourself mate. We've got a lot to talk about," added Hatchet Willis.

Blair saw no point in arguing or shouting out further, so he just lay there looking up at his two tormentors.

"I'm not gonna lie to you mate, I'm in a pretty bad mood," said Willis. "I mean, kicking the fuck out of you has helped a little, but I'm still feeling a bit grumpy. Your tough guy buddy - Mr. John 'Super Cunt' Kennedy - has wound me right up; the dirty mongrel."

Blair tried not to smile at this news, as it would have just meant more unnecessary pain and injury. He was pleased that John had pissed him off though, as this meant it was more than likely he was still alive.

"The plan for today was to carve that cunt up in his flat, then come back here and take a day or two killing you nice and slow. Fletcher here was really looking forward to it."

Fletcher smiled down at Blair, indicating that he had indeed been looking forward to torturing Blair to death.

"I underestimated that Irish prick the last time we tussled. Three of us went up against him armed with blades, and myself and Fletch ended up with fucking limps, plus I got a scar on my face.

Now, I actually like the scar on my face; I think it's pretty bloody cool lookin'. We could have done without the limps though - hobbling round like a pair of old cunts.

My knee hurts when it rains and I have to put my leg out straight to sit on the bloody dunny. It's a pain in the fucking arse.

Old Beanie was a bit luckier; he only got his face fucked up and had to get his fingers sewn back together. Point is, I know this cunt doesn't fuck around.

So today we went in eight-handed, with axes, hatchets, machetes and a double barrel bloody shotgun. The cunt's still alive!

I was there and I still don't know how the fucking mick did it - luck of the Irish maybe. He cost me five of my men though and that cannot stand. I've got such a hardon for him now you wouldn't believe it.

There is no bloody way on this earth that cunt gets out of Australia alive. No chance. I'm gonna cut his heart out and eat it."

Fletcher sniggered at this point; amused by both the vicious intent and the fact that he knew Hatchet Willis meant this literally and not just figuratively.

"Our little drug war has been an inconvenience and I could do without it," Hatchet Willis continued. "That's why I was gonna kill you and as many of your men as I could get my hands on today. But war or no war, John Kennedy was the one I really wanted. He's fucked me again, but it's the last time, I'll tell you that.

So you and your boys have got lucky. You don't die today and neither do they. You might end up wishing you were dead, but we're not gonna kill ya.

And your gang I don't give a fuck about. I can kill them whenever I feel like it. Right now I want the mick.

Northern Ireland, Ireland, I don't even know what the fuck that is - bombs, fields and arseholes. All I know is, he talks like a cunt, he's a dirty fucking mick and he's gonna die for days when we get our hands on him.

You and your boys get one more chance because of that fucker. You bloody tell him that he is never leaving Australia alive.

You tell him we're going to kill him and his mick bitch so slowly they're gonna think it's a career. You tell him we're gonna run a train on his woman and fucking ruin her; smash all her bloody doors in. You tell him I'm gonna fry his cock in a pan and feed it to him with some peas and mash.

Tell him I can't wait. Tell him it's the only thing I give a fuck about, till I watch him die. And of course, be sure and tell him what we did to you. And you be sure and tell him it was his fault.

Tell him that it's on him, just like what's going to happen to him and his mutt."

Blair didn't say anything and just continued looking up at Hatchet Willis and Fletcher. The thought of what they were going to do to him was now paramount in his mind and he was petrified at the possibilities, although he concealed it as best he could.

"Cat got your tongue, pretty boy?" asked Fletcher, standing on the kneecap he had previously stomped on and forcing down his body weight on it.

"We need to hear you say it mate," said Willis. "Tell us you're going to tell him."

"Okay, I'll tell him," replied Blair, once again stifling a scream.

"Good boy; now for the fun bit. You see, we can't just let you go scot-free and we need a nice juicy story for you to tell Johnny Boy. Please forgive us for what we are about to do," Willis joked, causing Fletcher to chuckle.

Blair tried to keep his fear hidden, but he knew he was about to go through some sort of terrible ordeal. The Hatchet Mob had a well-known reputation for doing horrific things to their enemies.

"What do you say Fletch; shall we give him the choice?"

"I love the bloody choice," replied a grinning Fletcher.

"Okay Blair," Hatchet Willis continued, "it's time for Blair's Choice; a bit like Sophie's Choice, but without the Nazis. I take it you've seen Sophie's Choice?"

Blair didn't reply, but from the expression on his face Hatchet Willis could tell he hadn't seen the film and didn't know what he was talking about.

"Stupid fuckin' kid. Never seen Sophie's Choice? It's a classic. I suppose you like bloody Two Hands or The Fast and the Furious?"

Again, Blair didn't reply, although he did happen to like both of those movies.

"Well, Sophie gets a tricky choice in the film. She has to pick between her two kids, to decide which one gets murdered. Now, you don't have any kids, so it won't be that exact choice, but we do have another difficult choice we like to give people."

Despite his dire predicament and ongoing terror, Blair's thoughts once again turned to his friend and fellow gang member Terence.

Did they have him? And if so, were they going to give him Sophie's Choice?

Would they make him choose between his two daughters, to see which one would be murdered?

Fletcher seemed giddy with excitement, as the situation was being explained to Blair. Clearly they had given this choice to others before him and evidently it was so unpleasant that it made a violent, sadistic thug like Fletcher eager with anticipation.

"You're going to love this mate," said Fletcher.

He was still training his .38 revolver on Blair.

"I fucking guarantee it. You'll be thinking about it every night before you go to sleep for the rest of your life, however long that is."

Blair tried to emotionally detach himself as best he could, but he knew things were about to get very unpleasant for him and that he would perhaps soon wish they had just killed him.

Chapter Fifteen

The fluorescent lights were burning into Blair's eyes and he closed them to give them a reprieve. He also wanted to give himself a brief psychological respite from the terrible situation he found himself in and the potential horrors he was about to face.

What were they going to do to him?

He was lying on the ground of some private garage lock-up, where he had no chance of rescue, at the mercy of two of the most notorious and sadistic figures in the Sydney underworld. He could hear Hatchet Willis and Fletcher talking quietly to each other, although he couldn't make out exactly what they were saying; not that he necessarily wanted to.

He didn't know how to feel about John in this moment. Even though John was one of his best friends and someone he admired a lot and kind of idolised, these monstrous guys had made a point of telling him that everything that was about to happen to him was because of John; it was John's fault.

On the other hand, if it hadn't been for John's actions earlier that day, they would probably be in the process of murdering him and the rest of his gang.

In a way, it all depended on whether or not what was to come would be a fate worse than death. After they were finished with him, would he wish he was dead?

Even as he steeled himself for a terrible ordeal, he still had time, in his own mind, to spare a concerned thought for his friend Terence.

Was he okay? Was he alive? Would he have to make a Sophie's Choice between his two daughters?

Blair was, at heart, a very loyal and quite moralistic guy. Given the choice, he would probably rather make his own Sophie's Choice and take the punishment, than allow Terence to have to choose between the lives of his daughters.

Terence may have been all front and kind of a pathetic gang member, but he had always come across as a compassionate and caring guy, constantly worrying about everyone else and making sure they were all okay.

Blair felt it would be doubly cruel and unusual for anything horrific to happen to such a good-hearted, altruistic individual.

Blair opened his eyes again to see Hatchet Willis and Fletcher bearing down on him, under the severe fluorescent strip lighting above. They grabbed him and roughly flipped him over on to his front, slamming his elbows and kneecaps down on the hard concrete floor.

They both then stood over Blair, in his eyeline, looking down on him, as he arched his head up at these two vicious thugs.

"It's time to play Blair, my old buddy," announced Hatchet Willis.

He was grinning as he gazed down on his helpless prey.

Fletcher once again took out his .38 revolver and pointed it at Blair's head, while Willis opened up the right side of his trench coat to reveal the selection of blades hanging from the cotton hoops in the lining.

"Well mate, which one do you like the look of?" Willis jokingly asked.

He paused for a few seconds and pulled out a machete.

Fletcher kept his gun trained on Blair, as Willis crouched down beside him and grabbed his right arm. He then brought the machete in close to Blair, pushing the tip of the blade against his arm as hard as he could without cutting him.

Blair was just resigning himself to having his arm cut off, when Willis pulled the blade away from it and cut the elephant tape that was binding his wrists.

"Behave yourself mate," he warned, "or you'll get a .38 slug in your fucking head."

"Too right mate. I'll burst your head like a fucking watermelon if you make one wrong move. Don't even fuckin' flinch," Fletcher added.

Blair wasn't sure what was going on at this point. Why had they unbound his wrists?

"Okay cunt, it's time to roll the dice," said Hatchet Willis. "You get a choice between the devil you know and the devil you don't. If it makes it any easier, they're both devils, so they're both no fucking good."

Fletcher chuckled at this, but kept his eyes and his gun focussed on Blair.

"I hear you do a bit of boxing Blair Boy. Are you southpaw or orthodox?" asked Willis.

Blair didn't reply, as he felt that no answer would help his plight at this point.

"Cat got your tongue eh? Fletch, you've seen the fucker scrap. Is he a lefty or a righty?"

"Definitely right, Hatch. I saw him floor one of our boys with a right hook."

"Floored one of our boys with a right hook? We can't have that. Nah, we'll have to sort this out."

Willis reached out with his right hand, as he stood over Blair, and opened up the driver's side door of the car, just beside Blair's head.

"This is it mate," explained Willis, "you can put your right hand all the way into that door jamb and hold it there, while I slam the fuck out of the car door.

I'll tell you now, I won't stop slamming it till your right hand is like an empty washing up glove. And if you try to pull your hand out before I've finished, you'll get your other choice as well; double trouble.

Now your other choice is the mystery box. I won't tell you what it is until after you've chosen, but I will tell you that if you choose not to put your hand in the door jamb, you'll end up wishing you bloody had."

Fletcher laughed and was grinning like a Cheshire cat. Hatchet Willis seemed to be taking pleasure in the process too.

"Don't listen to Hatch, mate. A tough guy like you needs his best punching hand. Take the bloody gamble," said Fletcher playfully.

He was trying to complicate matters further for Blair, while simultaneously amusing himself.

"Stop fuckin' with the little cunt, Fletch. He's got a big decision to make. All I'll say is, Blair, if you do man up and put your hand in, I will mangle the fuck out of it - "

"Yeah, he'll Joe Mangel your fuckin' hand," Fletcher interrupted.

Willis sniggered a little, before continuing.

"Like I said, if you do put your hand in, I'm going to fucking ruin it, but that'll be it. I guarantee we won't do anything else to you.

It's up to you mate. Make up your mind fast. The broken hand train will be departing soon and you'll be sorry if you miss it."

"Tick-tock you fuckin' cock," added Fletcher.

Blair knew he didn't have long and the choice he faced was an awful one.

Could he force himself to hold his right hand in the door jamb of the car and keep it there while Hatchet Willis destroyed it?

The other side of the argument was that he did kind of believe Willis - that this would be the end of what they would do to him today.

He was also convinced that the mystery option could well be even worse for him.

Hatchet Willis and Fletcher stood over him while he struggled with the choice they had given him, Willis mockingly warming up and stretching his right arm, as if preparing it for the workout of smashing Blair's hand in the car door jamb.

Fletcher was clearly enjoying proceedings too, but not so much that it distracted him from his primary role at this point, which was keeping his gun trained on Blair, ready to open fire on him if he made a wrong move.

Blair started to raise up his right hand, from his position lying face down on the concrete floor, aiming it towards the car door jamb.

"He's going for the door jamb mate," said Willis, enthusiastically tapping Fletcher on the shoulder.

At the last second though, Blair realised he couldn't do it. Part of him knew that he probably should, but he just couldn't bring himself to hold his right hand in place while they destroyed it.

He retracted his hand and placed his right elbow back down on to the concrete floor.

"Oh, that was close," said Willis. "Couldn't bring yourself to give up your wanking hand, eh mate?"

"I think you made the right choice mate," laughed Fletcher.

So that was it; he had made is choice.

What was the mystery option that he would now have to face?

He knew it was going to be awful, but he did his best to keep some sort of control of his fear and his emotions.

As this torment was progressing, he could have cried. He didn't want to give them the satisfaction though. No doubt tears from their victim would have brought them even greater amusement.

As he lay there on the cold, hard concrete floor, preparing for the worst, an abrupt knock came at the door of the lock-up.

Hatchet Willis made his way calmly across to open it, as if he had been expecting someone.

He opened the door narrowly at first, making sure the knock had come from the person he'd anticipated.

"Come on in mate, you're just in time," was his friendly greeting.

Another member of The Hatchet Mob had arrived to join in, thought Blair.

As the door opened wide and this person entered the lock-up, Blair turned his head to see who had come to join this torture party.

He had to squint slightly, because of the flash of sunlight mixing with the already harsh light from the strip lighting above. As it became clear who it was, Blair could not have been more shocked.

Chapter Sixteen

What is worse than being kidnapped and worse than being threatened and tormented? What could be more awful than facing beatings and torture from two sadistic monsters?

Betrayal from someone you trust and consider a good friend. Being stabbed in the back by someone you thought was a good and caring person and who you would have been prepared to take a bullet for.

That's what Blair thought anyway, as he struggled to cope with the realisation that one of his own guys had sold him down the river, served him up along with John and Lisa to their enemies and forsaken his gang as a whole.

Terence came strutting into the lock up, like he owned the place, with an unashamed grin on his face.

"G'day Blair mate. You lying down there for a bit of a rest are you?" Terence joked.

"What the fuck Terence? How could you mate?"

Terence made his way across the room until he was standing over Blair, beside a gun-wielding Fletcher. Hatchet Willis locked the door again and then walked over to join them.

"How could I what mate? Fuck you over? It was fuckin' easy, you stupid cunt; too easy.

You're no fucking gang leader. You're bloody dreamin' mate. Fair enough John and fair enough Peter, but you? Fuck off.

Plus I seem to remember something about you threatening to kill me over where I choose to stick my dick. I fuck who I want, when I want. Just like I'm fucking you right now.

Besides, I've been playing all you cunts from day one. I sew the seeds mate. I pull the bloody stings and make you all dance. I know you didn't take me seriously Blair, so now I'm moving up in the world."

"That's right Blair," added Hatchet Willis. "Meet El Tel, my new lieutenant. The Hatchet Mob is going to own this city, and your gang is over, one way or another."

"You're a sneaky, pathetic little cunt Terence! You're the lowest mongrel cunt in the whole of bloody Australia!"

Terence stopped grinning for a second and kicked Blair hard in the face, catching him in the mouth. He felt the dull thud of Terence's boot impacting on his upper lip and then came the warm metallic taste of blood filling the inside of his mouth.

Blair spat out the blood at Terence's feet and repeated his sentiments.

"You're a low cunt, mate."

This was typical of Terence; getting enthusiastically involved in the violence, in a situation where he was sure he couldn't be hurt. He was weak and cowardly, but he never missed a chance to act like he was some kind of hard man, once he was positive he couldn't be shown up or found out as the weak runt he was.

On this occasion, he contented himself with one savage kick to the head of his helpless victim, only because he knew there was plenty more sadistic violence to come and he was eager to be involved.

"You blokes seem to be getting on like a house on fire," said Willis. "Terry, you got here just in time mate. It's time for Blair to take his punishment like a bitch. Let's get him up boys."

Fletcher gripped Blair's left shoulder with his left hand, pressing the revolver in his right hand firmly against Blair's temple. Hatchet Willis grasped his right shoulder and Terence grabbed part of his torso.

"Ready boys?" asked Willis.

The other two nodded and Willis counted down to a simultaneous lift.

"One, two, three!"

They hauled Blair to his feet, which remained bound with elephant tape. Hatchet Willis and Fletcher aimed him at the right side of the bonnet of the black Holden, before flinging him on to it.

The three of them then adjusted his position, so that his upper body was flopped on the car bonnet and his legs were standing in front of the right front wheel.

"Get the ropes, eh," Hatchet Willis instructed Fletcher.

Fletcher handed his .38 revolver to Terence, who stood at the front of the car, parallel to where Blair's head was resting, and aimed it down at his former gang boss. Hatchet Willis was behind Blair, holding him in position against the car.

The ropes were the kind that people use to attach things to a car roof, or hold an overly packed car boot closed. It took them a while to get Blair secure in the position they wanted, tying his hands individually with the rope, stretching the rope over the bonnet and securing it to the front left wheel of the car.

Blair was absolutely terrified at this point and did his best to bury his head, face down, against the car bonnet.

Terence noticed this and grabbed the back of his head by the hair, forcing it round to the side, so that Blair was looking directly at him.

"You don't want to miss anything mate. Don't worry, I'm gonna stay with you the whole time," said Terence.

He leaned down on the bonnet, so that his face was close to Blair's, holding his head so that it remained facing him with his left hand, and pressing the gun against the top of his head with his right.

Fletcher took up a position just behind Blair, while Hatchet Willis moved around beside Terence, wanting to be in Blair's eyeline while he spoke to him.

"You're going to really bloody regret not putting your hand in that car door jamb," he said.

NEIL WALKER

Chapter Seventeen

"Have you ever been in prison Blair?" asked Willis.

Blair was looking up at Hatchet Willis and Terence, but didn't answer. He was making a habit of not responding to his enemies during this ordeal, as he knew that nothing he said would make any difference.

"No, he's never been inside," Terence answered for him.

"You're lucky mate," said Willis. "A few months inside and you'd have an arsehole like a blood orange. You'd come out of jail and be able to park this car in your fucking arse!"

They all laughed at this remark, with the exception of Blair.

"Me and Fletch have both been inside," Willis continued. "We ended up having a great time, didn't we Fletch?"

"Oh yeah mate, we bloody loved it," confirmed Fletcher.

"You see, you've got to run the prison like you run the streets. You can't take any shit and you can't have any cunt thinking they can cross you or fuck with you.

Any cunt getting any ideas, you've got to break him in fucking two. Or more specifically, you've got to split him in fucking two. You can't kill 'em all, so you've got to find another way to fuck them. Open him up Fletch."

Fletcher didn't miss his cue and immediately began unbuttoning Blair's trousers and taking them down, along with his boxer shorts.

"He's got an arse like a fuckin' Thai girl, mate," announced Fletcher.

He stepped back and took a good look.

"Just the bloody job."

"Have we got anything to use for lube mate?" Willis asked Fletcher.

"There are a few tins of XXXX in the Esky. We could pour one of them on it. Or we could all just fuckin' spit on it, eh?"

"No mate, I don't want to waste the bloody XXXX. Spit will have to do if I can't find anything else. I'll have a quick look around."

Hatchet Willis began slowly making his way around the lock-up, inspecting it for something they could use. Blair now knew what was coming and was overcome with a crushing sense of dread.

He could feel his legs shaking, but he tried to control it as best he could.

Terence was still holding his head in place to the side and staring down into his eyes. Blair was sickened by this and by the realisation of who and what Terence actually was.

Terence was a lie - a scheming, Machiavellian manipulator. A sociopathic liar, who spent all his time and invested huge effort in making everyone around him believe he was a good, caring guy, just to trick them, use them and persuade them to do what he wanted.

Fletcher slapped Blair hard on the right buttock, as Hatchet Willis made his way back over to them with a grubby looking metal can in his hand.

"How about this boys? It's some sort of grease or something. I think it would work a treat, but I don't want us to end up burning our cocks or anything."

"Give it to me," said Terence.

He temporarily passed the gun in his right hand over to Fletcher and reached out to receive the dirty metal can, which had a wooden stick protruding out of its open top.

Fletcher leaned down over Blair, taking over from Terence, with his left hand holding Blair's head in position and holding the .38 revolver at his temple with his right.

"Ta mate," said Terence.

He held the grubby can in his left hand and stirred the contents with the stick in his right.

"Let's test this muck out. If it doesn't burn eyeballs, it won't burn cocks and balls."

The three of them laughed at this, before Terence pulled out the stick from inside the can, set the can down on the ground and reached the stick over to Blair's face. It was soaking with the dark, greasy substance and Terence forced open Blair's right eye, with the fingers of his left hand, and dropped a dollop of the dripping liquid into his eyeball.

Blair grimaced and tried to turn his head, but Fletcher held it firmly in place.

"Fuck you!" Blair shouted.

"He's fine," concluded Terence, "lube him up."

Terence knelt down, put the stick back into the can and stood up holding the can in his right hand. He reached out his left hand to take over holding Blair's head in position, freeing up Fletcher's left hand to take possession of the can of black sludge from him. Once he had the grimy can in his left hand, he passed Terence back the revolver with his right.

Terence once again looked down on the helpless Blair, training the gun on him. Fletcher began roughly slopping the dark, greasy substance down the groove between Blair's buttocks and up into his anus with the wooden stick.

Meanwhile, Hatchet Willis was limping across the room to an old, paint-splattered boom box stereo that was sitting on a cluttered table.

Blair was just lying there on his front, trying not to scream out, as Fletcher was prepping him with the oily stick.

He was looking up at a grinning Terence with his left eye, the right one still thick with grease and unusable at this point.

Hatchet Willis spun back around to face them, as music loudly broke the silence.

Blair didn't recognise it, as it was nothing like the kind of music he tended to listen to, but Fletcher looked up and reacted instantly.

"Great fucking tune mate! That is what I call some nasty fucking fuck music! I'm starting to get a chub on already!"

Hatchet Willis had put on the Metallica song 'Seek and Destroy' from the 'Kill 'Em All' album. Terence also reacted as if he was a fan of this song, although Blair knew it wasn't his type of music.

This tallied up perfectly with all of Blair's newfound realisations about Terence; everything about him was a calculated lie.

His main motivation now was to be accepted and held in high esteem by The Hatchet Mob and Hatchet Willis in particular. Pretending to like the same music as them would no doubt be just the first of an endless series of deceptions and pretences.

Fletcher put the grease can down on the ground at his feet, but far enough out of the way that it wouldn't get knocked over during the imminent proceedings. Hatchet Willis arrived back over at the car, taking a position to Terence's right.

"Are you sure this song is long enough mate?" Fletcher queried with Willis.

"It's about ten bloody minutes mate," he replied.

"Yeah, but still Hatch."

"Don't worry Fletch, I stuck it on repeat."

"You bloody ripper! Let's get cracking!"

"Okay mate, you kick off, then Terence can get stuck in."

"No Hatch, you go before me. I don't mind going last," said Terence.

He was once again trying to get in Hatchet Willis' good graces.

"No Tel, I always go last. You see, I got HIV inside, from the bloody needle. I don't wanna poz you boys up by mistake."

Terence leaned down, so that his face was right beside the face of his former gang boss. Fletcher unbuckled his belt in position behind the helpless Blair.

"HIV mate. You've got to love that," Terence taunted. "Who's the tough guy now? Who's in charge now?"

As Blair looked at Terence's face with his only functional eye, he tried to focus on his hate and anger, rather than his fear and dread.

Terence really is the lowest, slyest piece of shit that ever walked the earth, he thought to himself. In his head, he vowed that he would not rest until Terence had died the worst death he could possibly imagine at his hands.

Chapter Eighteen

John and Lisa had managed to get out and clear of the apartment building just in time, before the police had the area completely locked down. They had then made their way to Peter's house, which had remained empty since Peter's death in Manchester on New Year's Eve.

Peter had lived by himself in a decent-sized, relatively normal looking suburban house, so it was an ideal place for them to drop off the grid.

Of course, in Australia, only John, Lisa, Blair and the other members of Blair's gang actually knew he had been killed. There was also the possibility that Terence had told the members of The Hatchet Mob, if he had deemed it relevant. Peter's body had never been found and it never would be.

They had managed to get inside the house unnoticed, not long before the TV bulletins had begun, followed by the nationwide manhunt that was still under way.

John had done a good job of getting rid of incriminating evidence at the crime scene, but the bloody massacre had happened in his apartment and he and Lisa were both being sought urgently by police for questioning. Lisa had lived there before and John was sure it hadn't taken much investigation for the police to get her name.

John felt that the police would struggle to make a case against them, based solely on what they presently had, as there were no witnesses and any finger prints or DNA inside the apartment belonging to him and Lisa could be explained by the fact that they had both lived there.

If the police managed to catch them, however, he believed that would be the beginning of the end. Someone had to go down for this crime and John and Lisa were the names in the frame.

Even though John saw everything he had done as being in self-defence, he felt that this would just get him a reduced sentence, rather than the freedom he felt he deserved. He had to keep himself and Lisa free and away from the police.

Hatchet Willis and a few of his known associates were also being sought in connection with the multiple murders, as the victims were all well-known to police as members of The Hatchet Mob.

It was John's belief that whoever the police could get their hands on first would get sent down for this crime.

There were too many bodies and the case was too high-profile for the police not to secure a conviction; they needed these murders to go from red to black on their homicide white board.

Peter had kept his house well stocked up with frozen, canned and dried foods. This meant that they hadn't had to leave the house in the week that'd passed since they arrived there.

The same went for Blair, who'd arrived at Peter's house on the late evening of the same day that John and Lisa had got there. John and Blair had not arranged or planned this, they had just both calculated the best location to head for, to lie low, after everything had gone crazy, and they had both come to the same conclusion.

Perhaps great minds think alike, or at least criminal minds think alike.

Even after Blair had informed John of Terence's treachery, and they considered the possibility that Terence would've told The Hatchet Mob about Peter's death, they both found it incredibly improbable that their adversaries would figure out that they were using his house as a hideout.

In the unlikely event that they did think of Peter's house as a place where their enemies were potentially lying low, John and Blair had reasoned that it would be too risky for them to come out in the open, make their way to Peter's house and search it, given the ongoing police manhunt.

To say that Blair hadn't been himself since he'd arrived would have been a huge understatement.

He'd been a shadow of his usual self - very quiet - and had kept himself to himself quite a lot, in the spare bedroom. The full details of his ordeal at the hands of Terence and The Hatchet Mob had gradually emerged, as the days had gone by, with Lisa proving to be an invaluable source of understanding and comfort to him.

Blair hadn't really talked to John much about what had happened to him or how he felt about it. It was too hard for him to open up to John, who he viewed as so strong and who he at times felt ashamed to even look at, after what had happened to him.

Lisa, on the other hand, had been through a similar ordeal to Blair. Plus, as she was a woman, Blair didn't feel as embarrassed to open up to her and she had encouraged him to do so.

Lisa knew how important talking about an experience like this was for the victim to come to terms with it. She also knew how vital a role empathy played in feeling like you were not alone, not guilty, and not less of a person, because you had been the victim of something horrendous like gang rape.

The only thing that had really lightened the sombre mood a little bit, during that week in Peter's house, were a few jokes and bits of banter about John being public enemy number one in Australia, with Lisa also wanted as some kind of gangster's moll.

There had been a number of tongue in cheek Quentin Tarantino references between the three of them regarding this.

Continued remarks about John and Lisa being like Clarence and Alabama in True Romance or Mickey and Mallory in Natural Born Killers had lifted the atmosphere somewhat.

Apart from this, it had been a dark time, with all three of them struggling to come to terms with what'd happened and contemplating what the way forward would be. What was their next move? What would become of them?

They couldn't hide out at Peter's house, sleeping, eating and watching DVDs forever.

After a week of mental and physical recovery, Blair had made it known to Lisa that he wanted to talk to John alone. As far as Lisa was concerned, any talking for him in his situation was good and she had made herself scarce and set up camp in the main bedroom, with the TV on and the door closed, while Blair joined John in the living room.

Blair had turned off the TV in the living room, to better facilitate the conversation he wanted to have with John, but had put some music on the main stereo, to make sure Lisa could not overhear.

The music came through the speakers at a moderate volume, as Blair sat down on the living room chair, at a right angle to John but facing him, as he sat in the middle of the three-seater couch.

John recognised the album right away; it was the Powderfinger album 'Internationalist'. Peter had been a huge Powderfinger fan and John had loved the band since his first time in Australia.

John sensed that this was not to be a music appreciation session, however, and that Blair had something serious he wanted to talk about.

"Terence, eh?" was Blair's opening remark.

"Little cunt," John replied. "I can't believe I was taken in by that piece of shit and his Mr. Nice Guy routine. 'Are you okay?' 'You know how I worry.' 'Do you want a line mate?' What a sly fucker. He's what we in Belfast would call a sleeked cunt."

"Yeah, that's one of the things that makes me most angry, at him and myself. Once you see how false and calculated all that bullshit was, you can't believe you ever fell for it. I mean, how did I ever believe anything that came out of that little cunt's mouth? Sly bloody poison dwarf."

"I know mate, but he fooled us all. You can't beat yourself up about it."

"Oh I have beat myself up about it, but next I'm gonna beat him up about it, and the rest. He's the worst excuse for a human being I've ever met and I'm going to make him pay."

John just nodded, but didn't reply to this. He was wary of getting into any discussion that would lead down the road to some sort of revenge plan.

John was furious and devastated by what had happened to Blair, but he still wanted out of the underworld life. He didn't want to jump into the deep end of some kind of blood feud.

"Do you think he's gay?" asked Blair.
"What?"

"Well, bisexual or whatever. Like, do you think he had some kind of thing for me and that was part of why what happened ended up happening? Are all three of them gay or bisexual?"

John paused for a few seconds, to contemplate his answer.

"Listen, there was a friend of mine in Belfast called Liam. He was a few years older than me, but we knew each other from when we were kids, right up through teenage years and so on. Now, as far as I knew, he was straight.

He dated girls at school and slept with them and everything. There were even a couple of times when I ended up dating girls that he'd also been out with.

Then there comes a point where he tells me he's bisexual and suddenly he goes cock crazy - no more dating women or even mentioning them. A couple of years after that, he comes out to me properly and tells me he's gay.

He had a really hard time coming out to his family though. There was even a time when he'd already come out to me as gay and we were both on a night out with his brother Johnny; I mentioned something about Liam being gay and Johnny immediately corrected me, saying, 'he's not gay, he's bisexual.' He obviously hadn't come all the way out to his brother at that time and I don't think he'd come out at all to the rest of his family.

I just had to back pedal like fuck and make out that I misspoke and I had meant to say bisexual.

Liam ended up going and working abroad, teaching English in countries like Germany and Poland. I think that was just to avoid dealing with coming out to everyone and handling the reality of who he was and what his family, and people in general, would think of that."

"Did he ever fully come out to everyone?"

"I don't know mate."

"How come?"

"We fell out."

"Oh yeah?"

"Yeah. I was with him in Belfast's big gay club, The Red Corner. He always wanted to go there at the end of nights out, so I'd go there with him, really just out of a sense of obligation.

Then, out of nowhere, he punched me full in the face - just a sucker punch, out of the fucking blue. Caught me flush on the jaw."

"Why the fuck did he do that?"

"For nothing, as far as I could see. I'm sure he had some drunken reason in his head at the time, but there was no disagreement, argument or fight.

Maybe I did or said something in my inebriated state that he wasn't entirely happy with. It doesn't matter what he thought was the reason to do it. Outside of a gym, wearing boxing gloves, you don't hit your friends in the face - ever."

"So what did you do? Did you take him apart?"

"No mate. You don't hit your friends in the face like that - ever.

I mean, he ran away after he did it and by the time I got my bearings after the punch in the jaw, I couldn't find him.

I've never seen him again, but even if I had've got him, I don't think I would've hit him. That was the end of the friendship though."

"So what about Terence then? Is he like Liam and he can't come out? Is he gay or bisexual?

Was he into me like that this whole time? Was the whole thing his idea, or was it Hatchet Willis' and he was just happy to join in?"

"Listen, after that incident with Liam, a lot of people I talked to about it thought that maybe he'd had a bit of a crush on me, perhaps going back to our teenage years.

They suspected that the unexpected and over the top act of violence, which seemed wildly inappropriate, was probably loaded with frustration that his feelings were unrequited, kind of like when little kids fancy each other and push each other over in the playground because they don't have any other outlet for their confusing feelings.

That theory kind of tied in with some weird behaviour that had been going on for a while. He'd been acting more like a jealous girlfriend than a mate, ever since he'd come out to me.

Maybe he'd even fancied me from the very time he started becoming attracted to other guys."

"Okay mate, no offence, but what the fuck does this have to do with anything?"

John chose to overlook Blair's rudeness - given the circumstances - and continue on to the point.

"Obviously there is nothing wrong with being gay or bisexual. Liam is gay and maybe he fancied me. Maybe Terence is gay or bisexual and he fancied you. That's fine.

But there is something wrong with sucker punching your good friend in the face, out of the blue, for some imagined slight, because you weren't happy with something he did or said or because he didn't reciprocate your homosexual feelings. And there is everything wrong with being a paedophile or a rapist. Terence is at least one of those, if not both.

Liam's actions were out of order and it cost him a friendship. Terence's actions were out of order beyond all measure, and they will no doubt cost him a lot more."

"Fuckin' right they were out of order. And you're spot on mate, his actions are going to cost him a hell of a lot more than a friendship. Little fucker."

"It was probably a bit of a power thing as well. You were his boss and are a lot tougher than him. Plus he's probably got that small man syndrome and he's trying to compensate for being so short."

"Yeah, he's only about four feet tall," Blair laughingly replied.

After they both laughed, there was a brief pause before Blair spoke again.

"I don't think I'll ever be able to listen to Metallica again mate," he said.

He was obviously feeling ready to joke about the situation a little bit.

"Not really your type of music anyway man," John replied. "Besides, Megadeth are way better."

They both laughed again, before Blair got on to the main order of business.

"I've been having a good think about our situation mate. I think we can sort everything out."

"Oh yeah?"

"Yeah. You see, we're both stuck; in fact, all three of us are stuck. You two are wanted like fuckin' Ned Kelly by the cops, plus you're being hunted by The Hatchet Mob.

I'm on The Hatchet Mob's hit list too and so are all my guys. If The Hatchet Mob doesn't kill me, they'll at least take away everything I've got.

And you and Lisa they'll kill before you can get out of Australia, if the cops don't get you first. We're all fucked. We're all stuck."

"So what are you thinking?"

"I'm thinking I've still got plenty of contacts. That money I'm getting laundered for you, I could get that washed into an offshore account in a false name.

I could then see to it that you and Lisa get fake passports in new names and that your new name matches the name on the offshore account.

Getting out of the country would still be a problem, because your picture will be all over ports, airports, stations; everywhere.

Every cop, or greedy fucker that wants the reward, will have their eyes peeled for your mug."

"So what do you suggest?"

"Did I ever tell you my uncle was a big-time sailor and fisherman?"

"I don't think so mate."

"Well he was. His mates used to call him Captain Jack; to me he was just Uncle Jack. He taught me everything he knows. With a half-decent boat, I could take anyone from anywhere to anywhere."

"So you could get us out?"

"For sure."

"You could hook us up with new identities, clean money and get us the fuck out of Dodge. That's great Blair!"

"Yeah, it would be."

"What?"

"That would be a big bloody job. I'm on a hit list for The Hatchet Mob and I'm in the middle of a massive bloody drug war. I'd need to clean house before I could help you out.

Once things get sorted out with the drug war, I wouldn't rest till I got you out and set you up for your new lives, you know?"

John did know. Blair was offering him a deal rather than just help. He knew it wasn't exactly a sly move though, as Blair really was in trouble and needed his help too.

"Quid pro quo," John replied.

"Eh?"

"I did Latin at grammar school in Belfast. It means I help you kill your cunts, you get me out of the country."

"I'm guessing that's a rough translation," Blair retorted.

He got the idea that John understood exactly what he meant.

"What about Lisa? I can't risk anything happening to her. I couldn't live with that."

"I've thought about that too mate. I've got a cousin in Perth. He's a couple of years older than me and he's into some shady shit over there.

He's got a big bloody house, with big grounds and security up the arse. I'm thinking we get Lisa set up comfortably in the back of a van and get a couple of boys I trust to drive her across the country.

They can take a route where they won't get stopped and even if they do get pulled over, she'll be well out of sight. She gets to my cousin's place, hides out living that Scarface life, and then once we're finished cleaning up in Sydney, I personally get you two the fuck out of Australia."

"Sounds like you've been doing a lot of thinking."

"I have."

"I'll have to talk to Lisa."

"Of course mate. She deserves to know what's happening."

Regardless of what Lisa said, John knew he had no choice and that she would just have to make her peace with it. Blair knew this too.

"So, when do we start?" asked John.

Chapter Nineteen

Lisa had not taken the news well. She was upset and frustrated that John was getting back into the drug gang scene and once again entering the violent Sydney underworld.

She'd been adamantly against him getting caught up in this drug war before they got to Sydney, but after they'd talked it out for a day or two, she'd come to accept it as the only realistic option they had to get out of their current predicament.

Lisa was now on her way to Perth, in the back of an air-conditioned van that had been made very comfortable for her. She was being driven by two of Blair's dependable associates, who he'd known for many years and would have trusted with his own life.

This reassured John that they could be relied upon, with Lisa's life at stake, and faithfully entrusted with the mission of transporting her safely to Perth without detection.

Everything was arranged for Lisa's arrival and John was glad that she was out of the city and safe, before things started getting bloody again.

John, Blair and the rest of the gang had begun the night in the back room of O'Neill's Bar, clarifying the details of the plan, making sure everyone was up to speed and on point, and sorting out weapons.

There seemed to be an enthusiasm and eagerness among the gang members to get out there and reclaim their territory and status. John's only eagerness was to get the whole thing over with as quickly as he could and get out of Australia, before he and Lisa ended up in jail or dead.

Blair's plan was very similar to John's plan to bring down The Brotherhood in Manchester the previous New Year's Eve. They were aiming to hit all of the clubs where The Hatchet Mob had a foothold, in quick succession, on the one night.

John didn't bother pointing out to Blair that his plan to topple The Hatchet Mob owed a lot, in terms of inspiration and detail, to his own plan to take down The Brotherhood though.

Blair was the leader of the gang now.

Blair was in charge and John was fine with this; he was happy to be just another soldier.

Plus, this plan meant that the whole thing could be finished by the next morning, and he could finally get away from violence and move on with his life.

As soon as they walked through the front door of Spice nightclub, John had his business head on. All of his feelings about not wanting to do this kind of thing any more were gone. He had to do it and he knew how to do it. This stuff was second nature to him.

Spice was a notorious drug den and had a history of violence. It wasn't the type of nightclub that people would have referred to as 'a shithole', however.

On the contrary, the club was decorated in a flashy and almost glamorous way and the clientele didn't look too shabby either - in terms of how they were dressed anyway.

The place was already thick with drugged-up revellers, dressed to impress.

Everyone in John's posse had weapons on them, and there were more weapons in the cars outside. They chose not to bring guns into the nightclub, as that would have attracted too much attention.

It would have been overkill and word would have spread across the city more quickly than their wave of violence.

John had a set of nunchucks tucked into the back of his combat trousers and a butterfly knife squeezed down the inside of his right German army boot. Blair had got him his preferred weapons, the weapons he'd favoured since his youth in Belfast.

He had even ensured that the nunchucks were the wooden kind with rope in between the sticks, rather than the ones with a chain: Game of Death nunchucks, rather than Enter the Dragon nunchucks.

These were the same kind of nunchucks Alan had given him in Belfast when they were both getting trained up in their use.

John hadn't shaved in over a week and Lisa had given him quite a different haircut. She'd said she was trying to make him look like the lead singer from the band Travis, Fran Healy.

In a way, she had succeeded. John did look a bit like the lead singer of Travis now, if Fran Healy had grown taller, worked out a lot, got a bit of a tan and started sporting a stubble beard.

Ultimately though, the main objective had been achieved. At a glance, at night, or in a busy nightclub with flashing lights, John did not look like himself. After all, he was still very much being sought by the authorities in Australia.

They had a lot more manpower for this mission than they had when going after The Brotherhood in Manchester. Every member of the gang who was not dead or too badly injured to get involved was there; that meant there were eight of them, including John.

Eight men was a good number for this operation and they were able to have a system in place with scouts and didn't have to move in a pack like John, Blair, Peter and Alan had on New Year's Eve in Manchester.

They had one guy in place outside the front door, Spence, just far enough away from the bouncers that he didn't draw their attention. He had a mobile phone at the ready, just in case of unexpected visitors.

There was another scout just inside the front door, Smitty, staying close to the entrance, and another by the fire exit, Poots.

The others were slowly and carefully scouring the club for rival drug dealers, while John and Blair made their way up to the balcony area.

There were two reasons why John and Blair headed for the balcony. It was both to check this particular zone for The Hatchet Mob and to be able to look out with a good view over the club, see the rest of their guys and keep a check on what was going on.

As they reached the top of the stairs to the balcony area, John was straining to see the seated section at the back of it, where he had found Hatchet Willis and his lieutenants the previous Halloween. But as they made their way through the crowd, there was no sign of Hatchet Willis or any of his guys.

Blair was walking with a slight limp, as he had opted to bring in a crowbar as his weapon of choice and had it tucked into his boot and running up the inside leg of his combat trousers. They were both effectively wearing the same battle uniform, with combat trousers and army boots, topped off with a smart short-sleeved shirt to avoid any dress code issues.

John had thought it was a poor choice for Blair to select a crowbar as his weapon and tuck it into his boot, but he hadn't said anything. He was letting Blair call the shots, make the choices, and run the show.

Also, he was finding it increasingly difficult to talk to Blair and relate to him.

Of course, it was understandable that Blair wasn't himself, after what he had been put through at the hands of Terence, Fletcher and Hatchet Willis.

Having done a good search of the balcony area, they made their way back through the crowd to the edge of the balcony. This enabled them to look out, with the great view they needed, over the rest of the club.

They stood in this optimal perched position, looking out at the crowd with their eyes peeled for a while, before Mack caught John's eye.

After scanning a portion of the club, Mack was the gang member who had been tasked with checking the gents toilets, if they had no luck anywhere else.

Mack was making his way from the toilets to the staircase leading up to the balcony. John nudged Blair and subtly pointed at him, in case Blair had not noticed.

This meant one of two things: either Mack had checked the toilets, found nothing and was coming to let them know, or he had found the drug dealers they were looking for.

As Mack reached the top of the stairs and made his way round the edge of the balcony to where John and Blair were standing, they were both watching him, eager to hear what he had to say.

When he reached them, he leaned his head into the middle of the two of them and spoke loudly, to be heard over the techno music that had the club bouncing.

"I've found them!"

Chapter Twenty

John and Blair made their way determinedly across the dance floor, through the enthusiastic Friday night crowd. Mack had asked if they wanted him to come into the gents toilets with them, or indeed if he should get a few of the other boys as well, so that they could go in after these rival gang members mob-handed.

Blair had declined either offer of help and told Mack that he and John would handle them. Again, John was happy to just quietly go along with what Blair said and he did not miss the responsibility of being the one giving the orders. If Blair had gone the other way and opted to charge into the gents toilets of Spice with a small army of gang members for back up, he would have been even more content to go along with that instruction and perhaps even take a back seat, while some of the others got blood on their hands.

As it stood, he and Blair were both more than capable in these kinds of situations and the pair of them were carrying weapons.

Mack had confirmed that none of these guys were well-known, infamous members of The Hatchet Mob, so it would be the two of them versus four standard Hatchet Mob members who may well have been fairly new to the gang. Given that John had gone up against Hatchet Willis himself, plus two of his lieutenants, on his own in these very same toilets and come away unharmed, he was far from concerned about what the outcome would be this time.

The previous Halloween, Hatchet Willis and his two lieutenants, Fletcher and Beanie, had been more heavily armed than John, and had him trapped and cornered. John had still managed to inflict devastating injuries upon them and had dealt with them with relative ease.

As the two of them entered the gents toilets, the four rival drug dealers were lined up casually against the far wall and were clearly not expecting them. They didn't even seem to notice them come in and make their way towards them.

John had slipped into a kind of violent, emotionally dead autopilot as soon as they'd come through the door of the bathroom. He had his right hand on the nunchucks stuck in the back of his trousers, ready to use them.

Blair had grasped the crowbar from his boot into his right hand, just after coming through the door, and he was also ready for action.

The smattering of other male clubbers in the gents toilets all seemed to notice the crowbar, and the general bad vibes, before the members of The Hatchet Mob did and began heading for the doorway. Before the gang member standing to their far right as they approached became the first to notice them, the pair were almost on top of their prey.

The gang member on their far left as they advanced was the one who John was most directly closing in on, and he was taking a swig of neat bourbon from a wide bottomed glass as John pulled out his nunchucks.

With a single swift motion, John spun the nunchucks out and upward, crashing one of the wooden sticks into the base of the wide bottomed glass and shattering it into the gang member's face.

His mouth exploded with glass, blood and bourbon, before he dropped to the ground, while John held his left hand in front of his own face, to block any glass from hitting his eyes and indeed to prevent the wooden stick of the nunchucks flying back and hitting him.

Simultaneously, Blair crashed the curved end of the crowbar hard into the face of the gang member on his right, who had been just too slow to notice him approaching. The crowbar impacted around his temple, sending him slumping down the wall to the tiled floor, while the gang member to this victim's right made a move to punch Blair, before he was next on the crowbar hit list.

He was not quick enough and only ended up throwing himself into a hard, metallic blow from Blair's crowbar. This strike shattered his nose and sent blood flying out of his nostrils and tears streaming out of his eyes, as he dropped to his knees.

John spun the nunchucks back over his right shoulder, catching the bloodied stick under his right armpit with his left hand. He then struck a firm forwards blow with that same wooden stick, spinning it over his right shoulder and out, like a right cross, into the face of the last man standing. It impacted on his nose and mouth and John followed up with two more quick-fire nunchuck blows to his head, to ensure he went down.

They had taken their opponents down in seconds and now rained stomps and kicks down on the four of them, as they lay on the tiled floor, to guarantee they didn't get up.

They were not concerned about the clubbers who had fled the scene going and getting the bouncers, as even if they did, by the time the bouncers responded John and Blair would most likely be out of there. In any case, they had a six-man back up team spread out around and just outside the club, if they had to tackle the bouncers to make their getaway.

John began to search the floored gang member to his far left for drugs, money and weapons, assuming that Blair would do the same with the gang member lying to his far right, and that they would meet in the middle and then leave.

Instead, Blair took up a position kneeling over the gang member lying semi-conscious in front of him and forced the curved end of the crowbar into his bloody mouth.

"Bite that, you fucking cunt! Bite it, you Hatchet bitch, or I'll put it through your fuckin' brain!"

John was not expecting this and turned to watch, just as the floored victim clenched his teeth on the cold, dark metal of the crowbar.

With a bloodcurdling crunch, Blair then roughly wrenched it around in a circle. He did it once, then a second time. John winced as he listened to the cracking of broken teeth, the choking of gargled blood struggling to get loose and the sound of muffled screams.

He found this sickening and unnecessary, but chose to look away and focus on searching the other fallen rivals. Blair was the gang leader now and it was his call. John would certainly not have stood for one of his guys second-guessing him in the middle of an operation like this, and he didn't want to do it to Blair.

"How do you like that, you little fucker? Your fucking gang is over!"

Blair then stood up, leaving his victim moaning and spitting up blood and fragments of smashed teeth. As he moved on to the next gang member in line - seemingly ready to do the same thing to him - John moved on to searching the next guy to his right.

They were interrupted when the door of the gents toilets was roughly flung open.

The pair of them spun round to see Mack bursting in with an urgent update.

"We've got a problem!"

Chapter Twenty-One

"Spence has gone! He's disappeared! All the guys are heading for the front door!" Mack shouted, with a sense of great urgency and concern.

Blair immediately spun around to the gang member he was standing over; the one who would have been next in line to have his teeth destroyed. He swung his crowbar upwards and to the side and brought it thumping down on to the guy's kneecap. This rival gang member yelled out and Blair quickly did it again, causing a fresh shriek that almost overlapped with the first one.

"Who took my guy? Where is he?" he asked the member of The Hatchet Mob at his feet, raising up his crowbar to threaten another blow.

John wanted to get out of there. They'd just about reached the end of the comfortable window of time that they had to do this and things had obviously gone wrong.

Spence had been stationed outside and wouldn't have left his post unless he had been taken.

It seemed that The Hatchet Mob were on to them and their whole plan was falling apart.

"I don't know! I don't know anything!" the Hatchet Mob member yelled up at Blair.

Blair cracked him again on the kneecap and shouted, "What is going on here? What is Willis' plan?"

"There is no plan! This is just a normal Friday night! I swear."

Blair reached down and yanked up the baggy trouser leg of the gang member's combat trousers. He then pushed the curved end of the crowbar up against the side of the kneecap he had been beating, stood his left foot on the guy's ankle and lifted his right foot over the back of the curved end of the crowbar, ready to stomp down on it with force.

"Tell me now, or I'm taking your fucking kneecap!"

"There's nothing, I swear! No one told me about any plan! Please don't take my knee!"

Just as Blair was about to stamp down on the crowbar and destroy this pleading gang member's kneecap, John grabbed him by his right shoulder and pulled him back.

"He's telling the truth mate! We need to go!"

Blair did not appreciate John doing this, but in that moment he realised John was right. All three of them made their way swiftly to the door and out into the main area of the nightclub.

As they dashed through the crowd, they actually passed the bouncers, who were charging the other way to get to the fight in the toilets and deal with the perpetrators. They had no time to appreciate the irony of this, as they got to the front door area as quickly as they could.

The other members of the gang were waiting for them near the door and Smitty - who had been stationed on the inside of the front door and had been the one to notice that Spence was gone - spoke up as they arrived on the scene.

"I stuck my head out to check on him a couple of minutes ago and he was gone. I had a bit of a look around, but no sign."

"Let's go," said Blair, gesturing for them all to make their way outside.

They quickly scanned the area around the outside of the club on foot, before getting into the two cars they had arrived in and beginning to drive around searching for Spence. It went unsaid that the plan they had intended to follow through with that night was now forfeit.

After nearly two hours of driving around Sydney, with all of them alertly on the lookout, wracking their brains for any reason he might have left - any reason other than that The Hatchet Mob had kidnapped him and were probably doing unspeakable things to him as they searched - they arrived back at O'Neill's Bar, to regroup and in the faint hope that he was there waiting for them.

As the seven of them entered the bar, they found that it was open, with the lights on, but completely empty.

"Harry! We're back mate!" Blair shouted across the desolate bar.

There was no response. It was very unusual for Harry to leave the bar open and unmanned like this.

Nate was the first to notice what was sitting in the corner of the bar where he and Blair would usually tally up at the end of the night and tapped his gang leader on the shoulder.

"Look mate," said Nate, pointing as Blair turned to face him.

In their traditional business corner of the bar sat two large, heavy-duty, black rubbish bags that seemed to be full to almost bursting point. They were sitting upright, supporting their own weight.

Noticing this, they knew something was wrong and each of them pulled out a weapon. John had his nunchucks dangling at the ready, as the group cautiously made their way to the other side of the bar to inspect the bags and check for intruders.

Blair set his crowbar down on the table, where he and Nate usually sat, and untied the top of the first bag. He immediately lurched back, giving everyone else a better view of what was inside.

The black rubbish bag was filled to the top with hacked up body parts, with a flick knife sitting on top of the bloody pile.

They all knew the flick knife was Spence's and realised straight away that this was what was left of Spence. Blair feared the worst as he opened up the top of the second rubbish bag and he certainly got it.

Resting on top of another pile of chopped up body parts was a familiar old watch. It was Harry's watch.

Chapter Twenty-Two

They had buried the remains of Harry and Spence before dawn, in a secluded place the gang usually reserved for burying the bodies of any enemies that needed to disappear. Spence's knife and Harry's watch had been placed in the graves with them and Blair had said a few words about each of them after the graves had been filled in, before they had left and headed back to the bar to regroup.

O'Neill's Bar was not a business that had ever needed security cameras, as either a deterrent or for evidence of fights, sexual assaults or robberies. Blair's drug business, however, was one than benefited from security cameras; not visible ones that would have attracted unwanted attention, but hidden ones, just in case.

The main reason for them was that, in the event that the gang were in the back room and there was a police raid, the cameras would at least give them a chance.

They would be able to move or destroy drugs, if they were holding them at the time.

The idea was that they would see the police come in on the TV monitor, which was located in the back room. Harry would stall the cops as long as he could, and they would be forewarned and gain valuable seconds to do what they needed to do. This had never happened though and O'Neill's had always proved to be a perfect cover for their operations.

Harry had made a habit of always starting the videotape - from the security camera feed - recording at the start of the night, when he opened the pub, and then taping over it the next day.

It had made him feel safer and as far as he'd been concerned, if the cameras and video equipment were there, he might as well use them. Not that he would have sent for the police if there'd ever been a robbery; he would have sent for Blair and the gang to go hunting for the offenders.

Harry had started the videotape from the hidden cameras recording as usual that Friday night and they'd captured what had happened in the bar.

Four guys with guns had come into the empty pub, snatched him and taken him away. Just over an hour later, they had returned and dumped the two black rubbish bags full of body parts in the bar.

They obviously hadn't taken Harry and Spence too far to do what they'd done, nor had they taken long to do it.

With ruthless efficiency, they had plucked these two guys from the world and then returned them in pieces a short time later. They had slipped up by not wearing masks or covering their faces though, and everyone in Blair's gang, including John, had taken a good look at all of the faces of the perpetrators from the video recording.

The following night was a manhunt. None of them had recognised any of the guys as members of The Hatchet Mob, but that meant nothing at the rate Hatchet Willis was expanding their numbers and territory. Willis was turning himself into 'the bank' and getting himself further and further detached from street level drug dealing.

This meant that his main role now was organising the supply of drugs for his gang members and taking in their money from his lieutenants, after they had collected it. It also meant that he was getting harder to find for the police and for his enemies.

Blair's plan was simple. They would find any or all of the guys in the video, kidnap them and make them give up all the information they had about why Hatchet Willis had done what he'd done, what his plan was going forward and where they could get their hands on The Hatchet Mob en masse.

Blair had split his guys into three groups, one group of three and two groups of two. Blair had paired himself with Nate, who seemed to be back in place as Blair's right-hand man, while John was also in a group of two, paired with Mack.

While Nate had never technically lost his role as Blair's lieutenant in the gang, John had been in position at Blair's side since agreeing to help with the drug war and would have expected that to continue.

John suspected that this slight downgrade in his status was because he had stopped Blair in his tracks, when he was interrogating the rival gang member in the gents toilets of Spice. He didn't really care though.

His level of prestige within the gang was not a priority for him; he just wanted to be out as soon as possible. The gruesome level this drug war was now being fought at only exacerbated the urgency with which he wanted to be done with the drug world and get out of Australia.

John and Mack had been sent to Kings Cross, probably the most dangerous location for them, especially in a group of just two. Again, John wasn't sure if this was some kind of punishment from Blair.

He wasn't overly worried, however, as he was confident he could handle multiple opponents from The Hatchet Mob and he had sparred with Mack before and knew he was pretty well trained up.

They had already searched one club and were walking through 'The Cross' to another. Wandering the street in Kings Cross had always depressed John, even when he had been in Australia the first time and wasn't involved in the drug business.

Maybe it was something about how close to the surface all the seediness of the area was. It was all right there for you to see.

Drug-ravaged teenage prostitutes would be trying to sell themselves to you. If you took them up on their offer, to basically let you do whatever you wanted to them for a fee, you would then take them into one of the grottiest hotels in the world and pay by the hour for 'sleeping facilities'.

There were places showing pornographic films on cinema screens, with older prostitutes moving through the crowd offering sexual services.

These vaguely described sexual services would ultimately be revealed, to anyone saying yes to the offer, to be a half-hearted hand-job in one of the upstairs rooms. No refunds were ever given, despite the almost one hundred percent rate of disappointment.

They wouldn't have to stay in Kings Cross much longer, as the mobile phone in John's pocket vibrated with a text-message.

John stopped Mack in his tracks, took out the phone and opened the message. It was brief and to the point.

'We've got one. Meet at the spot.'

NEIL WALKER

Chapter Twenty-Three

The spot Blair was referring to in the text-message was a secure storage unit, which John had originally started renting when he was first in charge of the Sydney gang and that Blair had continued using.

It had a lot of space inside and was mostly filled with bric-a-brac they would all leave there, lying scattered around or in crates, apart from on particular occasions when weapons, drugs or money would be stored there for short periods.

John and Mack passed Jason - one of the other gang members - on the way in, he having obviously been selected for guard duty. He was keeping watch outside the storage unit, just in case someone else happened by.

They entered the unit and closed the door behind them, seeing that the other four members of their gang were already inside with the hostage. The prisoner was tied to a slightly rusted metal chair and John immediately recognised him.

He was one of the guys from the video taken by the hidden security cameras who had been involved in the murders of Harry and Spence. They had obviously given him a bit of a beating, but John was sure the worst was yet to come.

"Alright John" said Blair.

His voice was stone cold and his eyes were filled with focussed determination.

"This cunt seems to be a little shy. Cat's got his tongue. I think you should get him talking."

Him get the guy talking? John was not expecting this. On the way there in Mack's car, he had been bracing himself for more crowbar cruelty from Blair, and was ready to be a spectator to the brutality, not the person responsible for delivering it.

Was this another punishment from Blair or some sort of test?

Maybe Blair was just showing him who was boss. Whatever the reason, John knew he had no choice and made his way casually across the room to where the hi-fi system sat, on top of a small table, surrounded by a mess of CDs.

As he flicked through the CDs, he posed a brief question to the group.

"Any wraps?"

Before anyone else had a chance to react or work out what he was planning, Mack spoke up.

"I've got wraps in the car with my kit. I'll go get 'em."

With that, Mack left the storage unit to fetch his boxing wraps, just as John found the album he was looking for. The hi-fi and the CDs had been purchased and put there by John when he had first hired and set up the storage unit.

John took the disc out of its case, slotted it into the CD player on the hi-fi and pressed play, before beginning to disrobe his upper body.

The first track came blaring out of the speakers and it was 'People of the Sun' by Rage Against The Machine. John had selected their album 'Evil Empire' for his interrogation background music.

He was going to emulate one of Doug's methods, which he had witnessed during his days as a member of The Brotherhood in Manchester. John planned to get stripped to the waist, wrap his hands - as if for boxing - and use this guy as a human punch bag.

Off the top of his head, this seemed like one of the least horrific options available to him, although it wouldn't exactly be pleasant for the victim.

In Manchester, when Doug went to work on someone like this, he would use the first Rage Against The Machine album. John had always preferred 'Evil Empire' and besides, their eponymous debut album was not there.

Also, when Doug used this technique on a rival, they would never be going to get away alive. John knew that this would be exactly the same in their current situation.

He hoped he wouldn't have to actually beat the guy to death and that one of the other gang members might shoot or stab him, after he had talked.

John started stretching and warming up to the sound of 'People of the Sun' and Mack returned with a rolled up set of white boxing wraps. John was used to using red Thai boxing ones, out of habit, but these ones would soon turn red with blood anyway.

As he unfurled the wraps and began wrapping his hands, he requested assistance from the others.

"Could you guys get him stripped? No point in leaving his clothes on and giving him a layer of protection."

Blair processed this request in his mind for a second, before giving his command to the others.

"Strip him guys."

Undressing the guy was awkward, as they already had him secured to the chair. All of the gang members in the room took to the task though, except John and Blair.

They tipped him in the chair, on to his side, and used their collective body weight to keep him secure while they untied him and took off his clothes, throwing down a couple of punches to his head and body as they did so.

John and Blair looked at each other without saying anything. If this was some sort of test and Blair thought John was going to flinch and fail, he was wrong.

John had his business head on and focussed on getting his hands wrapped.

By the time he'd finished wrapping his hands and the guys were ready to stand the now stripped and re-tied prisoner back upright in his chair, the CD had already moved on past 'Bulls on Parade' to the track 'Vietnow', which was half way through playing.

As John closed in on his human punch bag, he stopped short just before throwing his first punch. He saw something that he was not expecting.

The guy had a tattoo on his upper left arm that was now visible. It was a thick black number one with the words 'all for' and 'for all' circling it.

John stood back and dropped his arms, shocked by what he saw. He stared at the tattoo for a few seconds and then looked the guy in the eye.

"The Brotherhood."

John saw a glint of recognition in his eyes, before the guy looked down at the ground.

"I used to have the same tattoo myself; it was right there."

John leaned in closer to the guy and showed him the scar on his arm, where Simon had cut the tattoo off with his Stanley knife. The guy glanced at it, before looking down again.

John stood back up, glaring down on him.

"These are my brothers," he said.

The guy just kept staring at the ground, as if hypnotised by it.

"These are my brothers. Say it!"

John got no reaction and so unleashed a series of shovel hook punches into the guy's ribs; left, right, left, right. The guy screamed out in pain, as John stood back up straight.

"These are my brothers. Fucking say it!"

Again, there was no response.

"Say it you cunt!" shouted John.

He unleashed another flurry of hard and skilled shovel hooks into the guy's ribs.

The guy squealed in pain again, but still refused to speak or look John in the eye. After he stopped shrieking, the only sound left filling the room was that of Rage Against The Machine blaring from the hi-fi.

The others knew all about The Brotherhood and had an idea what was going on, although like John they were puzzled as to what a Brotherhood tattoo was doing on a drug dealer in Sydney.

John leathered punches into the body and head of the prisoner, until the white cotton wraps on his hands were red with dripping blood and his face and torso were also blood spattered. Still the guy wouldn't talk.

"Fuck this!" shouted John.

He crossed the room to where Blair had set down his crowbar and picked it up.

The guy looked on in fear as John marched back towards him with the crowbar raised in his right hand and his eyes filled with bad intentions.

"These are my brothers! Say it!"

John crashed the sharp part of the curved end of the crowbar down on the guy's bare left foot, which was tied to the chair leg. The guy yelled out in agony, as John followed up with a further two ferocious blows to the same foot.

"These are my brothers! Say it!"

The guy whimpered, but didn't speak, so John attacked the left foot again, this time focussing on the toes, with five savage strikes. The guy let out another anguished scream and then yelled, "Okay!"

"Say it," demanded John.

He dropped the crowbar to the ground.

"These are my brothers and this is my family. They can trust me with their lives and I can trust them with mine. To betray them is to betray myself and put my life in their hands - "

John then interrupted and finished it for him.

"I will give everything and more to uplift, protect and bring prosperity to my brothers."

John paused for a second and stood there, staring down at this bloodied mess of a Brotherhood member, before continuing his questioning.

"How? Who the fuck is running it? What's his name?"

The guy paused and John was unsure if this was an extra element of reluctance to give up information, or if he was just punch-drunk from all the blows to the head.

He did speak up after a few seconds though.

"Her name."

"What?"

"Her name; it's a she."

John was stunned.

"Kate?"

The guy nodded. John shook his head in disbelief.

"The bitch is back from the fucking dead."

Chapter Twenty-Four

Everyone started placing their hands on top of the hand of the person beside them, so that they all had one hand joining them to the person on their right and one hand joining them to the person on their left. Ray did likewise, with one of the Han brothers on his right and the other one on his left.

Even Burnum was part of the chain, as Kate sat down cross-legged on the large wooden table facing Ray and placed her hands, one on top of Ray's right hand and the other on top of Jake Han's left.

"Okay Ray, all I need you to do is listen to each line I say and then repeat it back to me. How about it Ray, are you ready to be one of us?"

Ray replied with an immediate, "Yes" and Kate began.

"These are my brothers…"
"These are my brothers…"
"and this is my family."
"and this is my family."

"They can trust me with their lives…"

"They can trust me with their lives…"

"and I can trust them with mine."

"and I can trust them with mine."

"To betray them is to betray myself…"

"To betray them is to betray myself…"

"and put my life in their hands."

"and put my life in their hands."

"I will give everything and more…"

"I will give everything and more…"

"to uplift, protect and bring prosperity to my brothers."

"to uplift, protect and bring prosperity to my brothers."

An enthusiastic round of applause was followed by a flurry of handshakes and pats on the back for Ray.

Kate had added another strong and eager young soldier to this incarnation of The Brotherhood. What Peter, Kate and Simon had started together in Australia, Kate had continued and improved on.

The Brotherhood in Sydney was growing in numbers and in strength.

The house was reasonably large and had room for them all to stay there, as and when they needed to. With eleven of them, including Kate, that meant plenty of bedrooms and living space. The large living room, where they had just sworn in Ray, was used in the same way and for the same purposes as the main hall had been in Nathan House in Manchester.

That Nathan House could only have been described as a mansion. The main hall within that house had been the most used room by the original version of The Brotherhood in Manchester. It'd been used for group socialising, some gang business and for swearing in new members.

This house was nowhere near as large and impressive as the Nathan House in Manchester, but it had been named after it. And the large living room had a number of the same items in it as there had been in the main hall in the original Nathan House. There was a large widescreen TV with a DVD player hooked up to it, as well as a PlayStation 2 and a VCR. The widescreen TV in the Australian Nathan House had Foxtel cable television with every available package of channels, including movies and sports.

The room also had two luxurious black leather sofas and one La-Z-Boy reclining chair, which was always in demand among the gang members, leading to many impromptu games of musical chairs, as anyone leaving the seat for even a short period of time would quickly have their comfortable position stolen. Just as Doug and Sanjay had done in Manchester, Kate, Peter and Simon had set it up as a place the gang members would want to be.

The three of them had selected this house, when they were initially making arrangements and organising The Brotherhood in Sydney, mainly for its size and the lack of nearby neighbours.

They called it Nathan House, with the idea that as they spread The Brotherhood to other cities and other countries, each one would follow the template created by Doug and Sanjay in Manchester and this included each chapter of The Brotherhood having their very own Nathan House.

As the rest of them prepared to celebrate Ray getting sworn in, with drugs, alcohol and partying well into Sunday morning, Kate signalled to Burnum, Jake Han and his brother Jeff with a firm nod of her head in their direction.

They discreetly left the others to it, made their way out of the large living room and went off to get ready for work. The four of them had some urgent business to take care of.

Chapter Twenty-Five

After burying the body of the guy they had learned was a member of the Sydney chapter of The Brotherhood and finishing the clean up process, John and Blair were exhausted as they returned to Peter's house in the darkness of Sunday's early hours.

They were careful to be quiet on the way in, as they were still very wary of drawing attention from the neighbours.

Just as John flicked on the light switch in the living room, he felt a strong choking sensation around his neck and his head jerked back, as he caught a glimpse of Blair collapsing forward on the ground unconscious.

John reached his hands up to his throat to try to release the pressure, but it was too late. Jake Han had him locked tightly in the slip noose of a heavy duty animal capture pole - a piece of equipment most often used by animal control officers, when dealing with violent or out of control dogs.

Jake was at the far end of the device behind him, with full control of the sturdy metal pole and he used it to force John to the ground.

Once down on his knees, finding it hard to breathe, John was able to look at everything in front of him and in his peripheral vision and assess how bad his situation was.

Sat on the living room chair was a casual looking Kate, swirling and nursing a brandy glass full of Hennessy as she looked down on him. He could tell it was Hennessy, as she had the bottle sat beside her on the chair.

In that moment, John couldn't recall if the glass and the bottle of Hennessy had been in the cupboard at Peter's house.

It was possible that she had brought them with her for effect, or just so that she could enjoy a relaxing drink in the dark, while she waited for her targets to come to her. Either way, he had more pressing matters on his mind.

As far as he was concerned, the fact that Kate was sitting there most likely meant death for both him and Blair.

Standing at the far side of the room, pointing a Beretta with a silencer on it at him, was a young guy of Chinese descent who he did not recognise; this was Jeff Han. His brother, Jake, was behind John, out of view, holding him in position down on his knees with the animal capture pole.

While the Han brothers were of Chinese lineage, they had both been born in Australia, with their parents being immigrants from Hong Kong. They had been heavily involved with Asian gangs in Sydney from their early teens and had a well-earned reputation for fearlessness and violence.

They'd both had quite an elaborate criminal career before hitting their early twenties, when Peter had recruited them to be his lieutenants in the burgeoning Sydney chapter of The Brotherhood. The promise of money, power and status had been enough to get their attention. Then tales of how The Brotherhood operated in Manchester, delivered by Peter, as well as by Simon and Kate when they were in Australia, were eventually enough to completely win them over.

Luckily for Kate, Peter had done such a great job of talking her up and preaching how integral to the organisation she was, they had gone along with her running things when she arrived back over in Sydney from England at the start of the year. Kate had also done a good job of making sure she kept them on side and she never tried to overly enforce the power of her leadership role over them. She had played it just right.

As Kate sat there, swirling her Hennessy in the brandy glass, and Jeff kept his silenced pistol aimed at John's head, a tall and well built Aboriginal guy came into view to John's right, having emerged from behind him.

He set down a club unlike anything John had ever seen before on the floor, well out of John's reach, and pulled a handful of cable ties out of the pocket of the black hooded top he was wearing. He then began using them to tie up an unconscious and helpless Blair, who had been knocked out by a single vicious blow to the back of the head delivered powerfully with his club.

This was Burnum, another face unfamiliar to John. He'd been working as a debt collector for a loan shark before Peter brought him into the Sydney chapter of The Brotherhood. Once he'd been sworn in as a member, he had seized the opportunity with both hands.

They were all tough and violent guys, but even among a group of hardened thugs like this, Burnum stood out as the hardest man in the gang. He knew this and completely played up to his role as chief gang enforcer.

The unusual weapon that caught John's eye was actually a time-honoured Aboriginal club, made from fire hardened mulga wood, with razor-sharp quartz set into the end of it with spinifex resin.

Burnum was not a particularly massive advocate of his Aboriginal culture, despite his traditional name. He chose to use this club purely out of respect for what a good weapon it was. He had yet to find a baseball bat or a cricket bat that could rival it, in his eyes, as a device for inflicting damage and pain.

John was in no way racist and had been a little shocked during his first stay in Australia at some people's attitudes and views regarding the Aboriginal people; Aboriginal Australians were mocked by some for being worthless, work shy, alcoholic bludgers.

At first, John would take people up on it and get into arguments over people making these kinds of remarks, but over time he had increasingly let it go. This was because the more time he spent in Australia and the more people he met, just about every Aboriginal person he came across seemed to more or less live up to this negative stereotype. Australian city centres would often have a scattering of Aboriginal alcoholics, wandering around having consumed too much grog.

John felt sure that there were many Aboriginal people who were nothing like this, but without positive examples to cite when arguing with these occasional racist comments, John ended up largely just ignoring them. Looking at Burnum though, John could tell almost immediately that this Aboriginal man was very different from any other he had encountered before.

He was muscular and obviously took good care of his body. His hair was fashionably cut and meticulously groomed; he had clearly taken his time styling it.

More than this, or his expensive looking clothes, John could just very quickly tell that this guy was on point.

Plus he knew that if this incarnation of The Brotherhood was anything like the one he'd been in when he was in Manchester, there would be no room for anyone who wasn't mentally and physically up to a very high standard.

Once Burnum had finished tying up the still unconscious Blair with the cable ties, he picked up his club and stood up. He then made his way over to John and took a position standing over him at his left side, with the weapon in his right hand, ready for use if needed.

"Hello John," said Kate, breaking the conversational ice.

"Fuck you," John defiantly replied.

Kate looked up at Burnum, who proceeded to push the razor-sharp quartz end of his club firmly into John's cheek. He kept pushing until John's head was tilted sideways in the animal noose and blood was running down his face from a small, quartz-induced wound.

Kate then gave him the nod to stop - for now. Burnum withdrew his club from John's face and once again held it at his side.

"Be polite Johnny Boy. After all, we're old friends. We've been through so much together."

This time, John didn't respond. He didn't see the point in getting his face cut again for talking back and realised that he might as well hear what she had to say; even if there was a chance it was just going to be a series of pre-murder taunts.

"Besides, we're going to have to learn to get along, now that you're going to be working for me."

John couldn't hold his tongue after hearing this remark.

"Working for you! Are you fucking kidding me?"

John instantly received a sharp blow to the back of the head for this, from Burnum's club. Burnum then went back to holding it by his side, staring down at John with dead eyes.

"You never learn, do you John? You never know when you're beaten. Jeff, call them."

Keeping his silenced pistol trained on John with his right hand, Jeff Han reached into his pocket with his left hand and pulled out a mobile phone. He then dialled a pre-programmed number and held the phone up to his ear.

It didn't ring for long before Jeff began speaking into it.

"We've got him. Put her on."

John was struck by a strong sense of dread as soon as he heard this. Before anything had been proved to him or explained in any way, once he heard the words 'put her on' he immediately got a sense of what they had done.

After a few seconds, Jeff made his way over to John and held the mobile phone to his right ear with his left hand, while pressing the silenced Beretta against his temple with his right.

A familiar voice came trembling out of the mobile phone.

"Hello. John?"

John's worst fear had been confirmed; it was Lisa.

Chapter Twenty-Six

John wasn't allowed to speak to Lisa for long, but she confirmed she was okay and that she hadn't been hurt. It was clear from the short phone call that she was terrified, however.

As Jeff Han stepped away from John, who remained in a forced position down on his knees, he put the mobile phone back in his pocket.

He then went back over to where he was originally standing, never lowering his gun from being aimed at John's head.

John was not likely to try anything at this point, as now he knew Lisa was at risk and that, in a way, her life would be in his hands.

Kate raised the brandy glass to her lips and took a sip of Hennessy. After she took the glass away from her mouth, she looked at John and spoke again.

"I can drink a whole Hennessy fifth. Some call it a problem, but I call it a gift."

John recognised this as the hip-hop lyric that Simon always used to reference when drinking Hennessy. It was from the Xzibit track 'Get Your Walk On', a piece of trivia that John knew because Simon had told him on numerous occasions, as he'd seemed to do with everyone.

He thought it best not to mention this and risk antagonising the situation further by bringing Kate's former partner into the discussion, given all that had happened in the past between him and Simon.

"You've got no idea how much I've been up your arse," said Kate. "Same with Blair. If anything, I've been even further up his arse. If I'd been any further up your arse and his arse, I could have brushed your fucking teeth for you.

I've been pulling the strings and watching everyone dance. Blair and Hatchet Willis are two fucking idiots. We've been playing them and their gang members off against each other for weeks, hitting one gang and making them think it was the other, stoking the fires of their fucking drug war and making it worse, without either of those two mugs realising what we were doing.

Now that they're all fucked up and chasing their tails, it's time to finish this and put them all out of their misery."

"How the fuck are you alive?" asked John.

He was no longer fighting the inevitability of their conversation in any way and was genuinely curious as to how she had managed to survive the shoot-out at Nathan House in Manchester on New Year's Eve.

"Coz your friend Ali is a shit shot; he couldn't hit a barn door with a banjo. And because your buddy Stuart is stupid cunt."

John didn't say anything at this point, but his face obviously gave him away when Stuart's name was mentioned. Kate smiled in recognition of this, before going on to explain fully what had happened.

"You see, Ali only managed to put a bullet just under my collarbone and it went clean through, although the force of it was enough to put me through the fucking window. Thank fuck for all the trees and bushes around old Nathan House, or I might have really hurt myself in the fall.

Don't get me wrong, I was bleeding from the bullet wound and the impact from the tumble knocked me out. But when I came round, Stuart had brought me in and treated the gunshot wound. If it wasn't for him, I might have bled out.

I always liked Stuart; we used to train together all the time. He was always too soft though. Once I was back on my feet, I did give him a reward. I sucked his dick...before I cut his fucking throat."

The others all sniggered at this, while John did his best to mask his anger and disgust.

"Thanks for the money, by the way John. If you hadn't left Stuart that nice pile of paper, I might have let him live.

As it was, that cash was just what I needed and it came in handy to get me to Australia and get me set up here. The Brotherhood was already up and running in Sydney and now we're all set to take over the city.

All we need is a little help from you Mr. Kennedy."

"What do you want from me?" asked John.

"Simple. I want you to do that thing you do. The Hatchet Mob have all but won this drug war, so now they have to go. I want those fuckers dead and gone, and you're gonna do it for me.

For now, Lisa is fine. We snatched her from the van and we have her tucked away where you won't find her. The guys who were driving her weren't so lucky.

She's under armed guard now, but she's being well looked after. That will continue, as long as you play ball. You have a week to scorch The Hatchet Mob off the face of the earth.

As for Sleeping Beauty on the floor there and the rest of your old gang, it's up to you. You can bury them or you can convince them to join The Brotherhood. Either way, what's left of their gang also needs to be over within a week.

If you follow my instructions and don't fuck around, you'll get Lisa back unharmed.

If you fail, or if you try to find her and rescue her instead of getting your job done, I'll have every guy in The Brotherhood go to work on her and then I'll slit her from her cunt to her chin and peel her open like a fucking peach.

Are we clear?"

John had sat and listened to what Kate had to say, keeping his mouth shut and his temper under control.

He'd taken on board what she'd explained to him and he understood his position perfectly, but now he just wanted to make sure she also understood her side of the situation they were in.

"You know me Kate, and you know I mean what I say. You also know exactly what I'm capable of. I'll do what I have to do and give you the city, if it gets me Lisa back.

That means I'm putting my trust in you and in The Brotherhood, because I have no choice. But all of you need to understand the outcome if you fuck with me.

If anything happens to Lisa, I will kill every single one of you. If you hurt her, I will kill you. If I help you and you double-cross me, I will kill you.

And it doesn't matter if you're the queen of the Sydney underworld, or if you have a hundred bodyguards. If I set my mind to it, I will kill you. I'll kill you all. Do I make myself clear?"

Kate smiled and took another sip of Hennessy. She was unfazed by John's threats and she knew she'd got what she wanted.

Chapter Twenty-Seven

John sat alone in the living room of Peter's house, having poured himself an extremely strong glass of Jack Daniel's Whiskey, with a dash of Pepsi as a mixer. He had set himself up on the living room chair, with the coffee table pulled over right in front of him. On the coffee table was a litre bottle of Jack Daniel's, a two-litre bottle of Pepsi, and his well-filled glass of strong Jack Daniel's and Pepsi with some ice.

During their conversation about Lisa and the terms and conditions of her release, Kate never mentioned the member of The Brotherhood who they had killed and disappeared that night. John hoped this meant that either she wasn't aware he was missing yet, knew he was missing and blamed some other enemy of The Brotherhood, or just wasn't sure what had happened to him and didn't want to reveal her uncertainty to John.

The situation was bad enough without it being exacerbated by their murder of a Brotherhood member.

John was just sitting there in silence, staring at the beads of condensation on his glass, when Blair entered the room. He had been in the bathroom cleaning himself up and tending to his minor head wound from the blow he received from Burnum's club.

Blair didn't say anything at this point. He just made his way into the kitchen, got himself a glass, put some ice in it from the freezer and came back into the living room.

He then put his glass down on the coffee table, walked over to the main living room stereo and started flicking through the CDs.

John did not react to any of this and just continued staring at his glass of Jack Daniel's and Pepsi. When Blair selected a CD, put it in the stereo and pressed play, John recognised the album right away. It was '1977' by Ash and the song that was playing was the first track 'Lose Control'.

This was not Blair's type of music, so it had clearly been put on for John's benefit. Also, Blair knew the multiple levels of attachment John had to the '1977' album.

Ash were a band from Northern Ireland, which made John like them more than most bands for a start. They were the same age as John and he'd seen them perform a number of times in Belfast venues like The High Wheel and The Spotlight, when they were still an unsigned band, gigging in small pubs and nightclubs, building a reputation.

The guys in Ash had named the album '1977' after the year of birth of two band members, which was the same year John was born. He had been in the same academic year as them, albeit at a different school in Northern Ireland.

The album title '1977' also referred to the year the first punk albums came out and the year of release of the film Star Wars. John chose to focus on the year of birth aspect of the title, because of the extra personal connection. Also, he was not a Star Wars fan, although he did enjoy punk music.

Blair had obviously put this album on as an attempt to cheer John up a little bit and as a kind of peace offering. Joining him for a drink may have had the same motivations, to an extent, although Blair also needed alcohol for medicinal purposes - to calm his nerves after the attack and dull the pain of his head injury.

He made his way back over to the coffee table, poured a strong measure of Jack Daniel's, followed by some Pepsi, over the ice in his glass, picked up his freshly poured drink and took a seat on the sofa facing John.

"Sorry about Lisa mate. How are you holding up?"

John paused, before finally looking away from his glass and up at Blair to engage with him in conversation.

"Fucked."

"I hear ya."

"What a fucking mess. I thought I could keep her safe this time. I'm a fucking idiot."

"Don't beat yourself up too much mate. None of us could have seen this coming."

"I suppose," said John, in a resigned tone.

Blair reached into the pocket of the board shorts he had changed into and pulled out an envelope, which he threw over to John. It landed on John's lap and he slowly opened it up.

He pulled out the contents and had a look through the items. There were two passports with fake names, one for him and one for Lisa. Also there was the bank card and paperwork for the account that had been set up for John, in the fake name matching the one on his passport.

John could now become Mr. James Douglas and, if he ever got Lisa back, he could start a new life with her as his wife Mrs. Pamela Susan Douglas. John wasn't sure why she got a middle name and he didn't, although it was so far down his list of concerns at this time, he didn't even ask.

The bank balance was exactly what Blair had promised him it would be. Blair had been true to his word.

"I've got a boat organised as well man. Once we get Lisa, I'll get you guys out of Australia straight away. I'll sail you up to Papua New Guinea. From there, the world's your oyster. I should have told you sooner mate, but it's all sorted."

John gathered everything back into the envelope and set it on the coffee table, before picking up his glass and taking a big gulp of icy Jack Daniel's and cola. He then held it in his hand, as he nodded to Blair and swallowed his cold, alcoholic mouthful.

"Thanks Blair. It's good of you to do all that."

"Oh, no worries man. And listen, sorry if I've been acting a bit off with you. The whole thing with the war, The Hatchet Mob, Terence, all the bodies dropping and people getting hurt - my head's been fucked John."

"It's okay mate, I understand. You've been through a lot. And if I was you, I'd probably have been a little bit off with me too. I mean, you flew around the world to help me fight my war and then I knocked you back when you wanted me to fight yours. It was fucked up.

And I don't want to blame her, but I would have been straight in there - guns in hands - if it wasn't for Lisa. She thought if I got involved, it would end up getting out of control and swallow us up. Looks like she was right."

"We'll get her back man. Whatever you need, you've got it."

"Cheers Blair, that means a lot. What about the others? Do you think they'll be in?"

"Are you fucking kidding me mate? The guys all love you. They'd follow you right into hell, without even stopping to put on sunscreen."

John laughed.

"Cool. Taking down The Hatchet Mob in a week, with the numbers we've got, isn't going to be far off a trip into hell. What about The Brotherhood thing?"

"I'll sell it to them."

"Are you sure you want to do it?" asked John.

"The way I look at it, I've got no choice. None of us do. Even if it didn't come down to Lisa or us and you having to come at us, we'd still end up dead as things stand anyway. There's no way Kate wants the whole of The Hatchet Mob rubbed out, but she'd leave us walking around. At least if we're on the inside, we're alive and we might get a chance to bring down The Brotherhood. Plus, I always liked the tattoo; it's pretty fucking cool looking."

John smiled. He remembered how Blair had always mentioned how much he liked John's tattoo, in the days before Simon had cut it from his arm.

"So, do you really think we can take down The Hatchet Mob in a week?" asked Blair.

"We've got no choice man. We have to get it done and we will. They're all dead; they just don't know it yet."

"Good. I owe those cunts. I want to dance on their fucking graves."

"I swear, if I can just get us out of this alive and get Lisa back, I will never hurt anyone again. No more fucking violence, from that moment until the day I die."

"But you're so good at violence."

"Fuck that. If we survive this thing, I'm gonna take up flower arranging. I'm gonna start saying sorry to cunts that bump into me in the street, or in bars, even though it was their fault. I'm going to be quoting the Buddha to guys acting like wankers, or throwing their weight around, rather than just knocking them out."

Blair laughed at this, like it was the most absurd thing he'd ever heard. John was not joking though.

"What's our next move?"

"Tomorrow we gather the troops and start the hunt."

"What, the hunt for Hatchet Willis?" asked Blair.

"No, Hatchet Willis is flying too low to the ground these days. Tomorrow we start the hunt for Terence."

"You bloody ripper."

Chapter Twenty-Eight

The search for Terence had begun on Sunday afternoon, but they didn't have any success in the hunt until Tuesday night. This was not surprising, as in the drug world Sunday and Monday were very often referred to as 'the lost days'.

They would end up as lost days because Saturday night activities would run into Sunday morning and sometimes Sunday afternoon and evening. Then Monday would inevitably disappear in a haze of sleepy recovery.

John had reasoned that Hatchet Willis would be virtually impossible to catch out in the open, given the current situation with the drug war. Terence, on the other hand, was just cocky enough to still put himself out there and think he would be okay.

Also, when paying people to have an eye out for someone, Terence was extremely easy to describe to those who didn't know him. You just had to tell them to be on the look out for a mini-gangster.

The instruction to those not familiar with Terry was to find a guy carrying himself like he was the world's hardest and most powerful man, even though he was little over five feet tall and had the physical build of a boy in his early teens.

Terence was easy to spot, in theory. Sure enough, after a couple of days of searching, he had eventually been sighted.

He was out for a drink on the Tuesday night in Bar Espana, probably trying to wash away a lingering comedown using alcohol.

John wasn't sure why the place was called Bar Espana.

It didn't seem to have a particularly Spanish or European feel or decor, apart from the sign above the door, which was painted in Spanish colours. He gazed at the illuminated yellow and red sign at the front door, through the windscreen of the car.

He had a mobile phone resting on his lap for updates, with the ringer volume turned right up and the vibrate function switched on. John did not want to miss anything.

Smitty was the gang member who was in the bar, discreetly keeping an eye on Terence. He'd been selected as the person best able to keep a low profile and avoid alerting El Tel, as obviously Terence knew all of them well, having previously been in the same gang, and if he were to see one of them watching him, he might bolt.

Having had a clean shave for the first time in about two years and worn a Stone Roses style bucket hat, which partially concealed his face, he didn't really look like himself at a glance. Given that Smitty was adept at blending into a crowd and not drawing attention, and that Bar Espana was always busy, they were confident that he wouldn't be spotted. Plus they knew that Terence was likely to be a little dazed and confused from drugs and alcohol and not at his most observant.

Smitty had a mobile phone at hand, to keep John abreast of anything noteworthy happening with Terry. There were two other gang members in the car with John - Poots and Jason - while Blair, Mack and Nate were back at the storage unit, getting set up and ready to go to work on their old mate, once he was delivered.

They had been waiting in the car for a long time, just staring out silently. This gave John plenty of time to reflect on Terence, someone who he would once have called a friend.

Just like Blair, John had been completely convinced by his act and had believed his false persona to be genuine the entire time he'd known him. He had certainly not seen his betrayal coming.

Now that everything had come to light, John was utterly sickened by him. John had bought into his fake Mr. Nice Guy personality and looked after him during his time in charge of the gang in Sydney.

The rest of the gang had done this as well, and had continued to take care of Terence and believe his lies after John had left Australia.

A person like Terence makes you hate them, when you finally realise what they are. More than that though, they really make you angry at yourself for ever believing anything they had to say, or buying into their constant lies and fabricated personality.

John was not a religious man - quite the opposite. He didn't believe in Christianity, but he was aware of the detail of the religion, having been taught Christian mythology as fact during his schooling and upbringing in Northern Ireland.

In Christianity, the Devil is sometimes referred to as The Great Deceiver and Terence had made John see why the worst imaginable creature was given this label.

Much worse than being a cunt was being a sleeked cunt, thought John.

John was angry with him for the lies and deception. More than that, he was furious with him for what he'd done to Blair and for almost getting Lisa and him killed.

If it was possible, Blair was on an even higher level of fury and disgust when it came to Terence. What he'd done to him could not be undone. John had little doubt that Blair would take an element of pleasure in what would have to be done to their former friend.

It was almost closing time when the mobile phone exploded with intense vibrating and a high volume, shrieking text notification sound. It was a text-message from Smitty - their man inside the bar - saying only, 'He's coming.'

"Be ready lads. As soon as I make my move, pull up and we'll get this done," said John.

He got nods from the other two, before getting out of the passenger door of the car and making his way over to a point on the street where he imagined Terence would pass. He was confident he knew which way he'd walk and was positive that he wouldn't get a taxi. When you understand the nature of a thing, you know exactly what it's capable of.

Despite all the cash he made from drug dealing, Terence was still very stingy with his money. He was extremely fond of winning people over and then subtly letting them pay for everything, keeping them sweet with the odd line of crystal meth or cocaine, from the inevitable bag in his pocket.

On this occasion, he was out on his own, probably hoping to pull, as well as drinking away his comedown blues. If he had pulled, John would've received a text-message update informing him of this, so John reasoned that he'd be leaving by himself and walking towards him.

John stood behind a tree, on the blind side of where he'd be approaching. It didn't take long before Terence's child-size feet came walking up on John and he stepped out to reveal himself.

Initially, Terence tried not to look up and make eye contact with this large and imposing shadowy figure. He was in scared little man mode and tried to change his path slightly, to go around this person who had emerged from the cover of a large tree.

As John stepped sideways to remain in his way, Terence looked up to see who he was dealing with. Despite the new look John was sporting, to make himself less recognisable, he knew him straight away.

He looked shocked and terrified, in that first moment of realisation, before trying to mask it and put on an act in an attempt to save himself. He reached out his right hand to John, offering him a handshake.

"Good to see you John. I've been worried about you."

John held out his hand and took a step forward. For a second, Terence thought he might just get away with it and get out of this situation safely.

However, John retracted his hand, as Terence leaned in to shake it, and sent his right leg sweeping forward - hard and low.

The kick took out both of his legs and he slammed down sideways on to the concrete.

John then followed up with a hard stomp down on his head with his right foot, knocking him unconscious. The car screeched to a halt beside them and the two gang members who were inside got out and opened up the boot.

Just as this happened, Smitty - who had swiftly made his way out of Bar Espana, after allowing a reasonable amount of time for their target to get clear and be intercepted by John and his fellow gang members - ran up to join them.

In a matter of seconds, they quickly and efficiently got him taped up with elephant tape and put his unconscious body into the boot of the car, slamming it shut. After a quick look around, to make sure no one had witnessed what'd happened, the four of them got into the car and set off on their way.

The guy in the boot was their way in. He was the key to bringing down The Hatchet Mob. John only had four days left to destroy The Hatchet Mob and save Lisa.

This was a good start though. Now it was time to break Terence.

NEIL WALKER

Chapter Twenty-Nine

They needed information and time was a major factor. Terence had to be forced to talk as quickly as possible. They needed to take The Hatchet Mob by surprise and en masse. It was Terence who had to tell them where and when they could do this.

Blair knew him better than anybody, especially now that he had worked him out in full. He had long been aware of his hard outer shell covering up a soft and weak interior, but now he also knew about the sly, Machiavellian aspect of his personality and behaviour as well.

For Blair, it had been like the end of Fight Club, once Terence's betrayal had been revealed; he suddenly saw everything that had come before differently, and instantly understood it all perfectly.

He knew that Terence would have been obsessively worming his way into Hatchet Willis' good graces, since he had been made a lieutenant in The Hatchet Mob.

This meant that he would've made a point of keeping himself totally in the loop of the gang's plans and activities. Therefore, if anyone knew when and where to strike against The Hatchet Mob, other than Hatchet Willis himself, and perhaps Fletcher and Beanie, it was him.

Blair had been looking forward to this moment. He finally had him at his mercy and he was relishing what would come next. He had planned it out, step by step.

He'd sent John away, along with two of the other three gang members who had brought Terence to the storage unit. Jason had been selected to stay and had once again been stationed outside the unit, to keep watch. Inside the storage unit were Blair, Nate, Mack and a still unconscious Terence.

He had been positioned slumped forwards over a heavy metal table, which had been dragged into the centre of the room. His torso was lying on the table, with his hands cuffed to the table legs at either side, his head hanging off the front of the table and his legs dangling down at the back, his feet only just touching the ground.

Blair splashed Castlemaine XXXX beer into Terence's face, from the can he was drinking out of. He awoke abruptly and came around, trying to take in his surroundings and take on board the situation in which he found himself.

"G'day mate. Haven't seen you in ages," said Blair.

Terence had his head tilted up to look at Blair, who was standing directly in front of him. He could also see Nate and Mack, who were standing at either side of the table he was handcuffed to.

"Listen Blair, I'm so sorry about what happened. It wasn't me. The bloody Hatchet Mob made me do it. They would have hurt my family mate."

Blair laughed out loud at this attempt by Terence to talk his way out of trouble.

"Give it up mate," he said. "Your days of lying to me are well and truly over. I will never believe another lie that comes out of your mouth. I know what you are and I fucking hate you. The only thing that might save your worthless, pathetic, little dwarf life is the truth. For once, you are going to have to tell the truth. That's the only thing that's going to stop the horror show."

"Please Blair! I had no choice!"

Blair laughed again. Old habits die hard, he thought to himself. Terence was going to have to learn that he wouldn't be able to get out of this by telling lies and trying to manipulate him.

Blair slowly walked over to the side of the room, took hold of a fold-out wooden table and nonchalantly dragged it across the concrete floor, allowing the bottoms of the folded wooden table legs to scrape noisily along the ground, until it was right in front of Terence. He unfolded it and set it up a few inches from his head.

He then casually walked back to the side of the room, brought over an old, heavy looking leather bag, unzipped it and tipped out the contents on to the table. The wooden table was now scattered with a mix of rusty old tools.

"Grab another beer you two," Blair said to his two assistants. "And Nate, could you check the barby for me mate? I want her nice and hot."

It was only at this point that Terence noticed the shiny silver barbecue, quietly smoking in the corner of the storage unit. Nate and Mack both walked over to this corner of the concrete room, which was fully within Terence's view.

Mack knelt down beside the yellow Esky cooler that was sitting on the floor next to the barbecue. He opened the Esky and took out two cans of beer, before closing it again. Nate checked on the barbecue, before reporting back on its status.

"She's looking good mate," Nate announced across the room to Blair.

"Nice one mate," Blair replied, as he began laying out the rusty tools neatly across the wooden table.

Terence was panicking, as his imagination began to go haywire with ideas of what they might be about to do to him with all this grim apparatus.

"There's no need for this Blair. Just tell me what you want to know and I'll tell you mate. Anything you want. Come on man!"

"Okay," Blair replied, continuing what he was doing. "Where and when can we get our hands on The Hatchet Mob all together; all at once?"

"Oh, come on Blair. How am I supposed to know that? Hatchet Willis doesn't tell me anything. I'm the bloody new guy for Christ's sake."

Blair just grinned knowingly at the response, before lifting an old poker up from the now tidily arranged table of tools.

The poker had clearly once been black, but most of the paint was long gone, apart from a little bit on the rounded handle. The rest of it was a worn and world-weary looking grey.

Blair made his way over to the barbecue with the poker in his hand, as Nate and Mack made their way back across the room to stand once again at either side of the prisoner.

"You're going to talk to me," said Blair, sticking the poker firmly into the hot coals of the barbecue, before making his way back over to Terence.

"I can't tell you what I don't know Blair," he protested.

"They say revenge is a dish best served cold, but I like it better when it's fresh off the barby," was Blair's only response.

Blair leaned down, so that he was eye to eye with Terence. He then took a firm grip of the gold hoop earring in his ear and twisted it painfully, before tearing it right through his earlobe.

He yelled out in agony, as Blair stood up again with the bloody gold earring held between his fingers.

"Looks like we've got ourselves a screamer boys," said Blair. "Mack, give us a bit of music. We need to drown him out, if he's gonna scream like a bitch. There's a heap of CDs I bought specially for the occasion right there mate."

Mack made his way over to the hi-fi and opened up the case of the top CD in the pile of new albums that were sitting in front of it on the table. He then took out the shiny silver disc, inserted it into the CD player on the hi-fi and pressed play.

Knowing Blair's musical taste, Terence was expecting a techno mix album, from someone like Carl Cox or Darren Emerson, to come blasting out of the speakers. He was surprised when instead some heavy sounding guitar music broke the silence.

"You'll like this mate. I saw how much you enjoyed Metallica when you, Fletch and Hatchet Willis were going to work on me. Well these guys are even better. They're called Megadeth. John switched me on to them and I for one think they're much better than Metallica. If it wasn't for you setting me up with The Hatchet Mob, I'd probably never have given them a listen, so thanks for that."

Blair had bought six Megadeth albums in preparation for this. The first one in the pile - the album that was now blaring out of the speakers - was 'Countdown to Extinction'.

Blair was nodding his head in time with the opening track 'Skin o' My Teeth', as he scanned the tools on the table, deciding which one to start with.

He stopped short of choosing his weapon and looked up at Terence, wanting to say one last thing to him before the interrogation got under way in earnest.

"You're here till you break Terry, and I will break you."

Chapter Thirty

Terence finally cracked during the early stages of the sixth and final Megadeth album in the CD pile. He had held out for a number of hours and taken a lot of punishment.

In the end, Blair had pushed him to the limit of his endurance and got the all-important information on The Hatchet Mob.

They would be meeting their drug distributor in an abandoned warehouse, on the outskirts of Sydney, that Friday. It was now late morning on Wednesday, so they would have to quickly formulate a plan and get ready.

Blair was confident that John would be up to the task of putting together the tactical master plan they would need, once he gave him the information. John was an expert plan-maker and would often quote Friedrich Nietzsche in saying, 'A man without a plan is not a man.'

All members of The Hatchet Mob would be at this meeting to provide security. They would be armed and there would be a large armed contingent there with the distributor as well.

They could take them all in this scenario, but it would be difficult and bloody.

As things had intensified during the night in the storage unit, Blair, Mack and Nate had switched from beer to a combination of cocaine and Red Bull. The cocaine had been snorted in lines from the same fold out wooden table that'd also been used to hold the rusty tools Blair had been using to interrogate Terence.

They'd been taking a line of cocaine roughly every half an hour and they had each drank a number of cans of Red Bull. They had even snorted the bag of crystal methamphetamine they found in the pocket of Terence's trousers, to provide them with an extra energy boost.

Now that they'd broken him and had the information they needed, they could switch back to beer and ease up on the cocaine. Blair had even taken a packet of steaks out of the Esky cooler, along with three cans of Castlemaine XXXX beer. He had thrown the steaks on to the barbecue, which they had made a point of keeping lit.

Terence had been stripped of his clothes at a reasonably early stage in the lengthy interrogation process.

His trousers and underwear had been pulled off and Nate had cut off the clothes he was wearing on his upper body with a sharp knife, so that they didn't have to uncuff him.

His body lay limp on the heavy metal table, his heading hanging forwards off the front of it, his legs hanging down so that his feet were slumped, partially touching the sludgy pool made up of a combination of blood, urine, faeces and bleach. He had lost bladder control a long time previously.

They had poured some bleach on the puddle of his body waste and blood, to dull the stench from it while they worked. All three of them had a slightly reduced sense of smell at this point anyway, from all the cocaine and crystal meth they had snorted up their noses.

Blair made his way back over to him, handing a can of beer each to Nate and Mack and keeping one for himself. He then opened his can into Terence's face and shook it a little, so that it fizzed up and sprayed him around his nose, mouth and eyes.

He was a bloody mess at this point. His face was cut up and beaten to a pulp and his whole body was covered in lacerations and lesions.

He had passed out shortly after giving up the information, but the beer in the face woke him up again, back into his living nightmare.

What had actually made him talk was the threat of having his right eye burned out with the poker from the barbecue. Blair had referenced Terence putting the dark, greasy substance into his eye during his rape ordeal, as he'd held the poker in front of his right eye and talked about what he would do.

He'd since put the poker back in place among the coals of the barbecue, where it was getting back up to its previous red-hot temperature, underneath the sizzling steaks.

"Good to have you back Terry," said Blair.

His tone was chirpy and upbeat, in contrast to the tense atmosphere and gory surroundings.

"Mack, skip the CD on to the last track and put it on repeat would you?"

Mack made his way over to the hi-fi and did as Blair requested. The Megadeth album playing at this point was 'Killing Is My Business…and Business Is Good!' and the track that was now set to play on repeat was 'Mechanix'.

"Check this tune out Tel, me old mate. John told me all about this one. You see, Dave Mustaine from Megadeth started out in Metallica and actually co-wrote some of their early songs. Then they kicked him out for being too much of a wild man on the drugs and grog, so this tune was his 'fuck you' to them.

On Metallica's first album 'Kill 'Em All' they had a song called 'Four Horsemen', which was a rip-off of a Dave Mustaine tune called 'Mechanix'.

When Dave formed Megadeth and they recorded their first album, they put a version of 'Mechanix' on it that was much faster than 'Four Horsemen' and had his original lyrics.

There was nothing Metallica could do about it, coz Dave Mustaine had written the song in the first place. It was a great way to say fuck you. And now I can say fuck you to you Terry, you fucking cunt.

You guys used Metallica to fuck me. Now I use Megadeth to fuck you. I believe 'Mechanix' is only a short song, but don't worry; we've got it on repeat."

"Please mate, you got what you wanted," Terence mumbled through his broken mouth.

"That's where you're wrong mate," Blair replied.

His tone was now more serious and less playful.

"We as a gang needed the information you gave us. We got what we needed. Now I get what I want. This is my birthday and Christmas present all rolled into one, you piece of fucking shit."

Blair paused to take a swig of his beer, before putting it down on the wooden table, beside the blood-spattered rusty tools and the parallel lines of cocaine, and continuing.

"Here's what I want El Tel. I want to show you what it's like. I want to take that poker out of the barby and stick it right up your arsehole. You won't be shitting yourself again after that mate.

Then you'll probably want to pass out, so I'm gonna want to rub petrol in your eyes so you bloody can't. Then I'm going to want to kill you.

Not quick mind. I want to enjoy it man. I want a fucking good show."

Blair then picked up a pair of rusty hedge clippers from the wooden table and showed them to him.

"These are going to take your cock and balls off mate. Once I get them hacked off, you'll take a while to bleed out. The boys and me are gonna sit down and enjoy a tinny and a steak, while we watch it happen.

Of course, once the fun's over, we've got to clear down and get rid of your midget body. You know the spot we like to use to get rid of the bodies we create.

After that, we might have a little sleep, before we pay a visit to see young Hayley and Katlin."

"No!" Terence screamed out, as best he could.

"Yes Terence! Yes! We're going to take care of your two daughters, just like you take care of underage girls."

Blair had warned Nate and Mack ahead of time that this would be one of the last things he would say to Terence. Of course, they were not going to do anything to his five and eight year old daughters.

This was just a final way to torment him and ensure he died a broken and tortured man, with the maximum amount of guilt and pain possible.

Blair knew he would believe it as well, as these were the kind of grisly depths that Terence himself would be capable of stooping to, even if Blair and the others would not.

"Right guys, grab his fucking legs and pull them apart," said Blair, giving his instructions to Nate and Mack.

He then made his way over to the barbecue to retrieve the red-hot poker.

Chapter Thirty-One

John sat on the dusty floor beside Blair, just below the grimy glass window. They'd got there early and been waiting for a very long time, but it was all part of the plan.

Blair had gone straight back to Peter's house, after disposing of Terence's body, and told John the information that he'd given up during the interrogation. He'd also told him the gory details of exactly what they had done to Terence, which John had listened to, while doing his best not to give anything away on his face in terms of his reaction.

He was a little shocked and disgusted by how far Blair had gone, especially after Terence had already been forthcoming with everything they needed to know. He didn't want to judge him though, or be seen to be criticising him or disapproving of his actions.

After all, while Terence had also betrayed him, he had not sadistically raped him along with Hatchet Willis and Fletcher.

Only Blair knew what that felt like and the damage that it left: physically, mentally and emotionally.

The abandoned warehouse was nothing more than a big, unswept, forgotten, empty space. There was a high roof and a decent square footage inside it, although it was not so large that it made John, Blair and the gang's task more difficult. They didn't want too much space for their targets to spread out into.

There was an upstairs office, which was situated up a metal staircase in the middle of the warehouse. It had windows looking out over the large interior area and had obviously been the manager's office, when the place had been in use. Now it was where John and Blair had set up to wait for their quarry to arrive.

Hatchet Willis and The Hatchet Mob were meeting their drug supplier from Brisbane to re-stock. Apparently, they did this every couple of months.

Terence had told Blair everything he knew about the drug supplier, which wasn't all that much. All he'd really known was that he was Greek, he was dangerous, and he had a lot of soldiers.

Both Hatchet Willis and this Greek drug supplier liked to turn up mob-handed and heavily armed for these transactions. This helped John and Blair, in the sense that it gave them the opportunity they needed to take out The Hatchet Mob en masse.

The tricky part was that they'd have to take on a large number of armed men, from both The Hatchet Mob and the drug supplier's gang, and there were only seven of them.

John had a well thought out game plan though and they were ready to put it into action.

John had come up with the tactics and Blair had handled logistics. Blair had really come through and used all of his contacts to get everything they needed to pull this off, and he'd done it in a massive hurry.

Some of the items had been relatively easy to get, like the petrol, the automatic pistols and the scrambler motorbikes.

More difficult had been the seven bulletproof vests, the Uzi .9mm submachine guns and the two-litre glass carboys that sat beside Blair and John, as they waited in the office of the warehouse.

These large glass containers were filled with John's petrol mix. They'd got everything by the Thursday night, giving John enough time to meticulously measure out and blend together the ingredients of the petrol mixture, getting just the right amount in each receptacle.

It was John's own recipe, involving white phosphorous, tar, palm oil, laundry detergent, petrol and the correct volume of air. Blair had been fascinated as he watched John do this and was tempted to ask him if this kind of expertise was standard in people from Northern Ireland, but decided against it, as he thought it might be offensive.

John and Blair were now lying in wait for The Hatchet Mob and the Greek drug supplier's contingent on the Friday afternoon.

They'd been in position for a couple of hours and their targets were due to arrive in the warehouse shortly. The rest of the gang were in place nearby - watching and waiting.

As far as Blair had been told, this was the first time that The Hatchet Mob and the Greek supplier's gang would be using this particular warehouse for their drugs for cash transaction. Terence had said that they changed the location each time, to make it less likely they would get caught by police or robbed by other gangsters.

This meant that John, Blair and the gang knew the terrain better than their enemies. They had been there the night before and again that morning, making sure everyone knew the layout and could visualise the plan.

John wanted nothing left to chance. This would be their one and only opportunity to take down The Hatchet Mob, or it would cost Lisa her life.

John sat fidgeting with his .45 automatic pistols, sliding out the clips full of bullets, tapping them on the ground, and sliding them back into the guns. He had four .45 automatic handguns with him and he went through this process repeatedly with each one.

Each time he tapped his spare clips on the ground, he did it in a similar fashion as well.

"You know that's the third time you've done that mate," Blair quietly pointed out, mindful of keeping his voice low.

"Well, you know me mate; I'm just itching to get my gun on," John joked, mirroring Blair's low speaking volume.

"You sure you're not nervous man? It's been a while since you've done any shooting."

"Are you kidding? I was made for this. I've said it before and I'll say it again, there's me and then there's Woody Harrelson - shit man, I'm a natural born killer."

Blair laughed.

"You're wanted by the cops like the bloody Natural Born Killers."

This remark tickled John, just as these types of tongue in cheek comments had done on a number of occasions before, when John, Blair and Lisa had first been hiding out at Peter's house and the news had come through on television that he and Lisa were both wanted for questioning by the police.

"I'll just be glad to get this over with and get Lisa back."

"Do you trust Kate to keep her word?"

John paused for a second, before replying to this.

"I trust her greed and her shrewdness. There's no percentage in killing Lisa and she knows I would hunt her to the ends of the fucking earth.

Having said that, when we get the details for the meet - after we've killed these cunts - we should turn up mob-handed, with all the guns, just in case."

Blair nodded his approval.

"Sounds like a plan mate."

The metal door to the warehouse then noisily creaked open. John got up on his knees, facing the window, raising his head up just high enough so that he was peeking through the bottom of the large, grimy office window.

He watched for a few seconds, then got back down on the floor beside Blair and whispered to him.

"Hatchet Mob."

John got back up on his knees and watched The Hatchet Mob enter through the metal door and begin setting up for the large-scale drug deal in the middle of the warehouse, just below the staircase to the office where he and Blair were hiding.

There were a lot more of them than John had been expecting. They just seemed to keep pouring through the door. Hatchet Willis had clearly been extremely active in terms of recruitment.

There was no speaking or joking between the members of The Hatchet Mob; they were there on business and they knew what they were doing.

At a rough count, John estimated there were over thirty of them. Neither of them had been aware The Hatchet Mob had anything like this level of manpower, but John thought it best not to worry Blair and keep his concern at their numbers to himself.

After all, there was nothing they could do now. The plan would soon be under way, whether they liked it or not, whether they would survive it or not.

Besides, this was John's only chance to save Lisa and he knew it.

Both John and Blair started getting ready for action. John tucked two of the .45 automatics into the front of his trousers; just below the bottom of the bulletproof vest he was wearing.

He then started tucking the extra clips into his trousers, beside the pistols. He picked up his other two .45 automatic pistols and held one in each hand, fingers on the triggers.

Blair slid his Uzi .9mm submachine gun over by the door, followed by two extra magazines filled with bullets. He then tucked his Beretta automatic pistol into the front of his trousers, as John had done with his two .45 automatics, just below the bottom of the bulletproof vest that he was also wearing.

Blair then carefully pushed two of the large glass containers full of petrol mix over towards him, so that they were sitting at either side of him on the floor, ready for him to lift when the moment came, one with each hand.

There were another two glass carboys full of John's petrol mixture, which he would leave in the office and quickly come back for, once the action had started and the first two had been used.

A few minutes later, the metal door to the warehouse creaked open again and John cautiously got up on his knees and looked through the bottom of the dirty window again. A sea of Greek guys in suits came flowing through the door.

It was time.

There were at least as many soldiers in the Greek contingent as there were Hatchet Mob members. John, Blair and the others would be badly outnumbered, much more so than they had anticipated.

John remained confident that his plan of attack was a good one and that there was a big advantage in having the element of surprise on their side. Still, taking on this number of armed gangsters with a team of only seven of them was a huge undertaking and a deadly risk.

John slid back down and nodded to Blair. Again, he saw no point in alarming him and alerting him to the odds, which were a lot worse than expected. It would only dent his morale and would serve no useful purpose.

They both shifted along the ground over to the door of the office, Blair with his two petrol mix containers at his sides and his Uzi within reach, John with his two .45 automatics in his hands.

Blair checked his watch. They would have about two minutes before the rest of the gang arrived and all hell would break loose.

He looked at the second hand ticking around the face of the watch, counting down the seconds to a bloody gunfight to the death.

Chapter Thirty-Two

Lisa had been awake for a while now; long enough to have given up struggling.

Her wrists were tied to the wooden bedposts tightly with cable ties, as were her ankles, but every time she awoke to this nightmare, she couldn't help but try to free herself. Her mouth was gagged with some kind of cloth and her trousers and underpants had been removed upon arrival and replaced with a disposable adult incontinence nappy. Obviously her captors did not want to have to deal with her needing to go to the toilet.

She was petrified and, day after day, her mind had been racing with the possibilities of what might happen to her next. When the door opened and three smug looking men entered the small bedroom, she feared the worst.

She had been held at the mercy of four of John's gangland enemies before and had been gang raped and abused mercilessly for hours.

Now she was struck by the sinking feeling that she might be about to go through a similar ordeal.

She did not recognise any of the three guys as they entered the room, looking down on her and grinning. One of them was clearly an Aboriginal man and the other two appeared to be Chinese. It was Burnum and the Han brothers, coming to carry out Kate's instructions.

Burnum took his quartz tipped traditional Aboriginal club from the inside pocket of his green army jacket and reached down with it, firmly touching the tip of it against her left foot. He then scraped it along the inside of her left leg, as he stepped round to the side of the bed and slowly made his way forward to where her head was resting.

Lisa was trembling a little, despite her best efforts to control herself. Burnum glared down on her with his usual dead eyes, as his club grazed along her inner thigh, moving upwards.

Although he was pressing quite firmly on her flesh with the quartz tip, he was not pressing so hard as to draw blood. Lisa could not really get a good look at exactly what he was doing; such was the position she had been tightly bound in.

When he reached the adult incontinence nappy she was wearing, he pressed even more firmly on it with the tip of his club than he had been pressing on her legs. He focussed on the part of it that rested on top of her vagina.

"That's it, squeeze the juice out of it mate!" Jeff Han laughingly interjected.

Jake Han sniggered at this remark, but Burnum did not react at all. He just continued to stare down at Lisa, with the expressionless eyes of an approaching natural predator. It was as if he was a shark and she was his helpless prey, floating in the ocean, unable to get away.

He continued past the disposable adult nappy with the sharp tip of his club, sliding it up the middle of her torso, as the Han brothers watched on from the foot of the bed. He stroked it over her throat, before pushing the quartz tip into the bottom of her chin.

"You don't move, you don't talk, you don't scream," were his instructions to her.

Given that she was bound to the bed and gagged, she didn't really see how she could break these menacingly explained rules even if she wanted to, but she nodded her agreement anyway. Burnum took on board her nod of understanding and compliance, but kept the club firmly pressed against her jaw, sinking it into the skin a little, but again not breaking the skin or drawing blood.

Jeff Han, who was still standing at the foot of the bed, pulled back the side of his nineteen-seventies style black leather jacket to reveal a black leather knife sheath attached to his belt, with a long and thick black knife handle sticking out of it. There was a leather clasp with a metal button on it, holding the knife in place, which Jeff popped open.

He slowly pulled the knife out of the sheath, as he gazed at Lisa. They were all leering down on her, Burnum still with the dead eyes of a psychopath, the Han brothers with the smiling glee of children about to open their Christmas presents.

Once the knife was out of the sheath, Jeff held it up by the handle, so Lisa could get a good look at it. It had a large blade, with one serrated edge and one razor-sharp edge.

The knife was actually an exact replica of the knife used by the character Rambo in the films, although not in the original novel First Blood by David Morrell.

Both Jeff and Jake Han had this exact same knife and they referred to them as their 'Rambo knives'. They were both enthusiasts of the films and the Rambo character and enjoyed the novelty of carrying these knives. They would even describe the knives as being 'perfect for killing gooks', with a smile of self-deprecating, ironic racism.

Jeff began spinning the knife around in his right hand, with skill and precision. It was spinning so fast at times that the blade became a blur, as Lisa looked on from her position on the bed, petrified.

With a final flourish, Jeff threw the knife up in the air and then managed to catch it by the tip of the blade in the palm of his right hand, dipping his hand carefully at the moment of impact, to mirror the momentum of the knife.

Without injuring his hand he then brought the knife under control, so that it was balanced in his palm standing up by the point. He held it there like that for a number of seconds, before he spoke.

"What do you think boys, could she take the whole handle?" he said, knife still carefully balanced in his hand.

"I'd say she could take two handles mate," replied Jake, pulling back his own leather jacket to reveal an identical knife hanging from his belt in an indistinguishable leather sheath.

Burnum did not look up to watch any of this, nor did he react or respond after Jeff Han had addressed the group. He just kept staring down into Lisa's eyes, holding the point of his club in position under her chin.

Jeff flipped his Rambo knife back up into the air by its point, so that it rotated in mid-air and he could catch it by the handle. Once he had the handle gripped in his right hand, he made his way from the foot of the bed and around the side of it, until he was level with Burnum.

Burnum stood up straight and stepped back a little, moving the quartz tip of his bat back slightly from Lisa's jaw. This allowed room for Jeff Han to move around Burnum, so that he was standing at the top of the side of the bed, looking down on Lisa's face, knife in hand.

At the foot of the bed, Jake Han unclipped the leather sheath on his knife and pulled it out by the handle.

He stood there with the knife at the ready, looking up at his brother, then down at Lisa, up at his brother, then down at Lisa.

Jeff took his knife by the end of the handle with his fingertips and dangled it over Lisa's face, occasionally touching her skin gently with the tip of the blade.

"If you shout or cry out, I'm going to cut your fucking face off and wear it as a skin franger while I skull fuck you," said Jeff.

This time Lisa did not nod up at her tormentor; she just lay there horrified. Jeff seemed happy enough that she would comply with the terms of his threat though, as he carefully slid the blade of his knife under her gag and cut it off, finally allowing her to breathe through her mouth again.

She gasped in a lungful of air, but did not scream or say anything.

Jeff nodded to his brother at the foot of the bed and he began cutting Lisa's ankles free, while Jeff cut her wrists free. Burnum just kept his eyes and club trained on her, from his position standing at the side of the bed.

Once they got her untied, they gave her a short time alone in the room, to take off the adult incontinence nappy that had been put on her and allow her to get cleaned up and dressed.

The clothes she had been wearing when she was kidnapped had been left there for her to put on, along with a pack of hygiene wipes and a can of female deodorant.

Burnum and the Han brothers then carefully marched her along the landing, down the stairs and through the door of the downstairs study, which Kate used as her office. Burnum guided Lisa in the door with a gentle shove and closed it behind her.

She was greeted by the sight of a woman of similar age to her, sitting in a leather chair, at the other side of the room facing her. She had a brandy glass with a generous measure of Hennessy in it in her right hand, and there was some rap music playing through the stereo, at a low volume in the background. The woman was wearing a vest top, combat trousers and trainers.

Lisa immediately noticed the membership tattoo of The Brotherhood on her arm, as well as the reasonably fresh looking, bullet hole sized scar under her collarbone. She had never seen this woman before, but she quickly calculated in her mind that it was Kate. John had told her all about this female nemesis of his, although up until this moment, Lisa had thought she was dead.

The woman - who Lisa believed to be the infamous Kate - smiled up at her from her seated position, swirling the Hennessy around gently in the brandy glass.

NEIL WALKER

Chapter Thirty-Three

"Hi Lisa, my name is Kate. Welcome to Nathan House."

Lisa didn't react and just stood there looking down at the seated Kate. She was doing her best to get her fear under control and steady herself. She also wasn't sure what to say.

"I thought us girls should have a chat. It's just us - no guards in here or outside the door. I'm unarmed, as you can see. All I have is this glass. There is no point in screaming for help, as there is nothing and no one near this house. And if you try to run or come at me, I will take you down, break the end off this brandy glass and use it to leave you with a face like Jigsaw. Do you understand?"

Of course, Lisa did understand the threat. She also knew exactly what Kate meant when she said she would leave her with a face like Jigsaw.

John had always been a big fan of The Punisher comics and had spoken to Lisa about them at length.

He had even made her sit through the movie version, starring Dolph Lundgren as Frank Castle a.k.a. The Punisher.

The movie had not featured the villain Jigsaw, but Lisa remembered John talking about him. He had waxed lyrical about how if they ever made a sequel to The Punisher, they had to include Jigsaw. John had even kept his Punisher comics from the nineteen-eighties in a ring binder, with each individual comic stored inside a poly-pocket for extra protection.

"The Punisher," Lisa replied.

Kate had not been expecting this. Very few women she'd ever met had been comic book fans at all, let alone knew the detail of a comic as obscure and violent as The Punisher.

"Very good. So you know you don't want to end up with a face like Jigsaw and you're going to behave?"

Lisa nodded.

"Okay, pour yourself a drink and sit down. Stop standing there like a cunt."

This whole experience had terrified and terrorised Lisa. She'd been taken hostage, witnessed the murders of the two guys tasked with transporting her to Perth, been drugged to knock her unconscious, woken up tied to a bed and gagged, been kept like that for an indeterminate amount of time, and been taunted by Burnum and the Han brothers. Now she found herself face to face with Kate, who she had heard a lot about - all of it bad.

Was she about to die? Was Kate just mocking her and amusing herself, before torturing or murdering her?

Lisa steeled herself as best she could in her mind, as she didn't want to show her disquietude if she could help it.

She made her way into the centre of the room, picked up the decanter filled with Hennessy - from the small wooden table in between Kate and the empty leather chair that was clearly where she was to sit - and poured herself a drink.

Lisa wasn't really sure what the alcoholic liquid in the decanter was or if she would like it, but she would drink it anyway. She knew alcohol would help.

Once she had a generous serving of Hennessy in a brandy glass, she sat down in the leather seat facing Kate and took a sip. It wasn't the worst thing she'd ever tasted, nor was it close to being the best.

"How's the Hennessy?"

"I'm usually a vodka girl, but it's okay."

"Yeah, it took me a while to get a taste for it. Simon loved Hennessy, almost as much as he loved rap music. Spending all that time with him, I eventually acquired a taste for both. You remember Simon, don't you?"

"Vaguely," Lisa replied.

She masked her contempt for him, and the traumatic memories that his name triggered, as best she could.

"He liked you," said Kate, with a wry smile.

They both took a drink from their brandy glasses, Kate sipping, Lisa almost gulping.

"Do you like hip-hop music?" asked Kate.

"Not really. I like a few of the big chart singles, like that Puff Daddy one, but it's not really my thing. A lot of it can be quite derogatory to women."

Kate sniggered at this somewhat clichéd point of view.

"I find it very empowering. It's real go get 'em, up and at 'em music. I think more women should get into hip-hop."

The rap album playing in the CD player was 'Devil's Night' by D12 and shortly after Kate said this, the line, 'I fuckin' hate you, I'll take your drawers down and rape you, while Dr. Dre videotapes you,' could be clearly heard through the speakers. It caught Lisa's ear and, given the context of the conversation, she did not feel at all empowered by this line.

"Do you really think rape is empowering to women?"

"Well, I felt incredibly empowered when I had you raped."

This shocked Lisa, to say the least. She had always assumed that Simon had been the mastermind of the terrible ordeal she had suffered at the hands of The Brotherhood in Sydney.

"Yeah, the whole Sydney operation was my idea; how to use you to break John, how exactly to go about breaking you. Everything. How is your snatch these days anyway? All healed up?"

Lisa was appalled and had no words. She just looked back at Kate and took another big drink from her glass of Hennessy.

"Maybe D12 isn't for you. Have you heard of that new guy 50 Cent?"

50 Cent had recently become a phenomenon in the music industry all over the world. Lisa had of course heard of him and nodded in response.

"Simon told me about him ages ago. He made an album a few years ago called 'Power of the Dollar', but he got shot nine times and the record label dropped him and shelved the album.

Simon had a bootleg copy of it though and thought it was the best album he'd ever heard. I think you'll like it."

Kate made her way over to the stereo and stopped the D12 album that was playing in the CD player. She then took a TDK C90 cassette out of its case, which had the album details and track titles written on the inner cardboard sleeve in biro, and slipped it into the cassette player, pressing play.

"Do you mind if I have another drink?" asked Lisa, as Kate made her way back to her seat.

"No, help yourself. You can pour me one too."

Lisa walked over to the table, poured herself a drink and then carried the decanter over to Kate and poured her one as well. She then placed the decanter back on the small wooden table and took her drink back over to her leather chair, once again sitting down to face her tormentor.

As this was happening, the opening of the album 'Power of the Dollar' had begun playing out through the stereo speakers.

The album opened with an introductory skit that had a little music in the background, before the first proper track. It contained the line, 'there are only two types of people in this world: winners and losers.'

"He's right you know," said Kate. "There are only two types of people in this world: winners and losers. Which are you?"

Lisa wasn't sure what to say to this or if the question was rhetorical, so she once again didn't reply and took a sip from her freshly poured glass of Hennessy.

"I'm a fucking winner. I don't know about you Lisa. John is definitely a winner, but I'm sure you already know that. That's why I wanted him working for me and why you're here, to properly incentivise him.

Around about now, he'll being going head to head with a couple of the toughest drug gangs in Australia. Either he'll kill them all and manage to stay alive, or he'll kill some of them and end up dead.

Hopefully he kills them all, coz that's less hassle for me. As long as he weakens my main rivals enough for me to take them down, I don't really care.

I am kind of curious to see if he can pull it off though."

Chapter Thirty-Four

The knock on the metal door of the warehouse was the signal, and John and Blair knew what was coming. Terence had told Blair that they always agreed a different knock at the beginning of each meeting, just in case.

As the knock came, in the format agreed upon by The Hatchet Mob and the Greek contingent at the outset, these two drug gangs remained calm, if a little irked that their business was being interrupted.

One member of The Hatchet Mob made his way over to the metal door of the warehouse, while the others looked on, impatient and eager to get the exchange concluded and extricate themselves from the situation.

John was watching through the bottom of one of the grimy windows in the office where he and Blair were hiding. Blair had his hand on the handle of the door, ready for them to spring into action at the exact right moment.

Beanie was the door opening volunteer from The Hatchet Mob and John recognised him from their altercation in the gents toilets of Spice nightclub the previous year. Even looking at him from a distance, through the bottom of a dirty window, John could not fail to notice the horrific looking scar on the side of his face, from when John had torn a hole in his cheek with his butterfly knife.

Within seconds of the metal door to the warehouse being opened by Beanie, the mood among those looking on, waiting to finish their drug deal, changed dramatically. The sound of a gunshot and the sight of an exploding head and spattering blood and brain pieces sent them all reaching for their guns.

Nate had got one of the guards to knock the door in the correct way, having made him do it at gunpoint. No doubt they went along with his instructions - to be quiet and for one of them to do the agreed upon secret knock - relatively readily, thinking that Nate had made a mistake, was out of his depth, and would be easily dealt with by the small army of gun-wielding drug dealers, once he got inside.

Immediately upon Hatchet Mob lieutenant Beanie opening the metal door, Nate had shot him in the left side of his head, at point blank range, with a .45 automatic, so that his lifeless body fell to the right, leaving the doorway clear. He then quickly executed the member of The Hatchet Mob and the member of the Greek gang, who had been on guard duty outside, in similar fashion.

The gang members inside swiftly drew their guns and prepared to fire.

As these rival gang members began firing on the main door area, Blair came storming out of the office door, on to the top of the metal staircase that looked down on them, and launched one of the glass petrol mix containers into the air above them.

John quickly followed him out of the office door, and on to the top of the metal staircase, with a .45 automatic in each hand. He fired a bullet from the pistol in his right hand into the airborne petrol mix container, when it was just a few feet above the gun-toting gang members.

When a fireball exploded over them, there was a break in the gunfire on the door, which enabled the members of Blair's gang, who had arrived on the scene at exactly the right time, to come tearing through the doorway on scrambler motorbikes in quick succession.

There were four of them on the motorcycles, wearing helmets and bulletproof vests, each of them carrying an Uzi submachine gun in one hand and steering with the other.

There was fiery chaos in the old warehouse, as the sound of gunfire reverberated from the walls and ceiling and gang members who had caught fire or been hit by bullets yelled out in pain. A second fireball exploded over the members of The Hatchet Mob and the Greek drug gang, after John fired a shot into another petrol mix container that had been hurled into the air above them by Blair.

Hatchet Willis limped determinedly through the fire, flames dancing on his back, pumping and firing his slide-action shotgun.

The four of Blair's guys on scrambler motorbikes were circling their adversaries and firing their Uzi submachine guns, corralling them in one area under John and Blair. Nate was also firing on them, with his .45 automatic, from just inside the main doorway.

Both the members of The Hatchet Mob and the members of the Greek drug gang were returning fire as best they could, but they had been ambushed with such swiftness, precision and savagery that it was hard for them to hold their own. They were going down in large numbers and many of them were on fire and screaming.

John made his way down the metal staircase, walking sideways so that he could fire at his targets with his two .45 automatic pistols simultaneously, as he came down to their level.

Blair hurled the remaining two petrol mix containers into the air above them in quick succession and John fired a bullet into each one, creating two huge fireballs that joined together in mid-air above the rival gang members, who could find no way to escape.

The shoot-out did not last long. John's plan had been executed perfectly and the members of The Hatchet Mob and the Greek drug gang stood no chance.

Soon they were making their way around the bodies strewn across the floor of the warehouse, putting a bullet in the head of anyone who wasn't dead.

Blair made a point of being the one to put the final bullet into both Hatchet Willis and Fletcher. Doing this gave Blair an instant sense of closure and satisfaction.

Thanks to the speed and accuracy of how they had put this well thought out game plan into action, none of them had been seriously injured. A number of them had taken hits in their bulletproof vests, but that just meant some painful bruising to the flesh underneath.

They took most of the drugs and money, leaving just enough so that when the police found the crime scene, they would most likely conclude that it was a drug deal gone wrong and that the members of the two gangs had killed each other. Perhaps, in time, they would even tie this drug gang massacre to the previous violent incidents of the drug war in Sydney - maybe even including the blood bath in John's apartment - and use it to close any open cases, blaming dead men for killing other dead men.

Once John was happy that the crime scene looked the way he wanted it to, that they had collected everything they needed, and that everyone on the ground was dead, they all left the warehouse. They then made their way back to the storage unit to regroup, stash the money and drugs, and contact Kate.

Chapter Thirty-Five

They had to wait until Saturday afternoon to be given a time and place for the rendezvous to pick up Lisa, having let Kate know about their successful mission on Friday by text-message.

The instructions were to meet beside a disused boathouse, which Blair told John was in the middle of nowhere. Blair had not even been aware of the existence of the boathouse, but he knew the area where the directions were telling them to go.

The message from Kate had said that John should arrive with Blair and the rest of his gang, but he'd told Blair he was willing to go alone, even though they had previously agreed to turn up mob-handed with all the guns, when it came time to meet Kate. However, Blair and everyone else in the gang insisted on going with him.

This was a relief to John, as he was sure that the extra guys and guns would help things go more smoothly.

He wasn't sure what Kate would do if they didn't follow her instructions exactly, but he felt obliged to at least offer to go alone, especially after they had already risked their lives in the operation to take down The Hatchet Mob.

It made sense for Blair and the others to go with him anyway, as they were now technically part of The Brotherhood and would need to meet their new gang and, at the very least, placate the situation with them. This meeting would be for show, as far as Blair was concerned, as both he and John were planning to go straight to the boat Blair had arranged for their escape, after the meeting with The Brotherhood, taking Lisa with them.

John had his and Lisa's new passports in one of the large pockets of his combat trousers, along with the bank card and paperwork for the account containing his money. He had made sure that the metal button on the pocket was firmly closed.

Blair had brought his passport, bank card and credit cards with him as well, also securing them in one of the large pockets of his own combat trousers. He was planning to stay with John and Lisa for a little while, at least for the first stop of their trip in Papua New Guinea.

John was fine with this. In fact, he was fine with just about anything, as long as the three of them managed to get out of Australia alive.

They'd travelled in two cars and had stopped for a while, a short distance before the deserted meeting spot, to get geared up. This meant that as they slowly drove towards the boathouse, they were all wearing their bulletproof vests and had guns at the ready in their hands.

The road became a dusty trail, which then opened out to a large space of empty and equally dusty ground with the old, rusted up boathouse behind it. The wind was strong enough to whip up a haze of powder in the air above this expanse of dry, sandy ground.

Although the air was thick with dust, as soon as they could see the boathouse they could also see The Brotherhood. They were standing a few feet from the side of the boathouse, with three cars in front of them.

They were all wearing long black leather coats, except Burnum, who was wearing his preferred green army jacket. It was clear that they had their hands on weapons concealed under their coats, but they had not yet drawn their guns.

As they pulled up in their two cars, around ten feet from the waiting members of The Brotherhood, John was struck by the mixed race nature of the Sydney incarnation of the gang.

Not that race was an issue for him, nor indeed had it been an issue for anyone involved with The Brotherhood in his time in the gang, but in Manchester they had all happened to be white, with the exception of Sanjay and Dave.

Almost half of this group appeared to be of Chinese descent, half of them were white and of course there was Burnum, who was of Aboriginal descent.

All of them recognised three of their waiting rivals, from the video that had been recorded in O'Neill's Bar the night that Harry and Spence were taken and killed. John obviously also recognised Burnum and the Han brothers, as well as The Brotherhood's female leader.

Kate caught the eye of a number of members of John's contingent. She stood out as a woman in a man's world and also caught the eye of these guys, as she was an attractive young lady.

Of course, she was as deadly and ruthless as she was pretty, and she was smiling as she watched the armed members of this rival drug gang pull up to a stop in front of her in their two cars.

As John and the others stepped out of the cars, wearing their bulletproof vests and with their guns held openly in their hands, the members of The Brotherhood quickly drew their weapons from beneath their coats and pointed them at these seven rival gang members.

John, Blair and the others followed suit, raising up their pistols and taking aim at the slightly larger armed group.

Kate was the only one who didn't produce a gun, although she did have one concealed under the long black leather coat she was wearing.

"Oooh, so exciting," she said.

"Put the weapons down and give me Lisa," John commanded.

"Or you could put your weapons down and then we'll give you Lisa," Kate laughingly replied.

There followed a period of tense stalemate, as they all aimed their guns at each other, simultaneously eager to pull the trigger and reluctant to open fire and cause a disaster.

"I suppose we could call this an Australian standoff," said Kate, breaking the silence.

This remark broke the tension a little and caused a few sniggers from her contingent, as well as a chuckle from Blair, who was standing at the opposite side of the car from John.

John gave him the side-eye of disapproval.

"Listen, do you see the car with the blacked out windows?" asked Kate.

John looked at the cars, then back at Kate.

"Yeah."

"Lisa is in there with a gun to her head."

"If you hurt her, you die."

"Oh grow up John. She's fine and she'll continue to be fine, if you guys put your guns down. Lisa is actually quite a nice girl. I don't know what the fuck she's doing with you."

This last remark brought a few more sniggers from her side of the Australian standoff. Blair made a point of not joining in this time, although he did find the quip a little bit funny.

"Are we supposed to trust you?" asked John.

"Well, either that, or we can just stand here for fucking ever, pointing guns at each other. It's pointless anyway. You know the drill; if you start shooting, she dies.

Besides, you've trusted me so far and everything has gone okay. I'm actually pretty happy with you motherfuckers. And all of you, except for John, are now joining The Brotherhood, am I right Blair?"

"Can't wait," Blair responded, with just a hint of sarcasm.

"You see John, we're all friends here. We're all brothers. I suppose I'm some kind of female brother or Brotherhood sister, but whatever.

I'll make it easy for you. We'll all put our guns down on the ground at the same time, nice and slowly. Then Lisa comes out, we give her to you, and we all shake hands and chill the fuck out.

Sound good?"

It did sound good. John looked at Blair and the pair nodded to one another.

"Okay, slowly put the guns down, on three," John replied.

He then began the count.

"One."

There remained a tense distrust, as they all kept their guns trained on each other.

"Two."

John was concerned that this might be a trick and that The Brotherhood would open fire on them at the end of the count.

But what other choice did he have, with Lisa being held in the car with the blacked out windows at gunpoint?

"Three."

After an added second of anxious pause, they all slowly lowered their weapons to the ground in tandem, setting them down cautiously on the dusty earth at their feet.

They then stood up to face each other.

"Okay, let me see her," said John.

Kate nodded to Burnum and he made his way over to the side of the car with the tinted windows and opened up one of the rear doors.

Lisa emerged, with her wrists bound behind her back with a cable tie and her mouth gagged with elephant tape, closely followed by Ray, the member of The Brotherhood who had been guarding her. He had left his gun in the car, in keeping with the ceasefire agreement brokered between John and Kate.

John was elated and relieved to see Lisa, so much so that he failed to properly take note of just how upset she looked and the fact that she was clearly trying to shout something through the tape on her mouth. As John ran to her and threw his arms around her, Blair and the members of his gang relaxed.

For a few brief seconds, everything was okay; everything was perfect. John held Lisa tightly in his arms, in a way that told her he never again wanted to let her go.

After this embrace, which felt to John like it had lasted for a long time, with the world falling away beneath them, John stepped back slightly and pulled the strip of elephant tape from Lisa's mouth, in one quick motion, to minimise the pain of tearing it from her skin.

"It's a trap!" she shouted, as soon as her mouth was free.

Immediately after this happened, the sliding metal door at the side of the large, rusted boathouse slid open to reveal ten guys wearing long black leather coats, training two pistols each on John and the others, one pistol in each hand.

Nate quickly made a move to grab his gun from the ground and they all opened fire on him. In a few seconds, he was cut to pieces by a hail of bullets, with most bullets hitting him in the head, arms and legs, while a few thudded into his bulletproof vest.

He collapsed in a pile of his own blood, as it sank into the dust.

This was followed by an uneasy interlude, as John, Blair and the others contemplated going for their guns. Poots was the one who couldn't resist the temptation and, in that moment, just could not bring himself to surrender to The Brotherhood.

As he dropped to his knees on the ground and grabbed his dusty Beretta, there was another eruption of gunfire, even heavier and more relentless than the previous one.

Bullets shredded his head, shoulders, arms and the upper part of his legs almost instantaneously, as well as a couple impacting on his bulletproof vest.

His torn and lifeless body fell to the ground, not far from Nate.

"That's enough!" shouted Kate. "Don't be stupid guys! Leave the fucking guns alone!"

The rest of them followed Kate's instruction, realising that it was pointless to follow in the bloody footsteps of Nate and Poots. The horrifying realisation of just how much trouble they were in now washed over John.

"Meet the Perth chapter of The Brotherhood," Kate proudly announced.

She then gestured to the firing squad behind her.

"G'day guys!"

This was the smug greeting from the member of the Perth chapter who was apparently their leader.

"W.A. all the way!"

Chapter Thirty-Six

He was going to die in some horrific way, as were the rest of them. In their own way, they all had it coming; they were all in the game and they all knew the risks.

Not Lisa though. She didn't deserve any of this.

All she was guilty of was falling for the wrong guy and now she was going to die for it. Maybe he could bargain in some way; offer to play along with whatever they wanted, if they would spare her life. He would try if he got the chance, but he doubted he'd be successful.

Only a matter of weeks ago, they had been having the time of their lives in Hong Kong. Sydney was only supposed to be a brief layover on their way to an amazing new life. Instead, the chaos had caught up with John once again and consumed both him and Lisa.

Then he heard footsteps closing in on him - multiple sets of footsteps, stopping right beside him.

He felt two hands roughly pressing down on his shoulders and another hand grabbing the top of the cloth hood that was over his head, ready to pull it off. They had come for him.

Now it was time to die.

The cloth hood was pulled off his head abruptly and the artificial light inside the boathouse dazzled his eyes. As his eyes adjusted, he could see that the boathouse didn't look quite so dilapidated and disused on the inside.

John could feel his legs being cut free and he was then lifted to his feet by the two men who stood over him, as they put their hands under each of his arm pits and jerked him upright, so that he was standing.

His legs were stiff and painful from the position he had been kept bound in for a couple of hours, but he managed to keep his feet. His hands remained tied with a cable tie, behind his back.

Looking to either side, to see who had lifted him up, he saw that they were both people he'd first met the night The Brotherhood got the drop on Blair and him in Peter's house. To his left was Burnum and to his right was Jeff Han.

Beyond Burnum, to his left, were Lisa, Blair and the others, all hooded on their knees on the floor and tied in the same way as John had been. John could see that the combined members of the Perth and Sydney chapters of The Brotherhood were beginning to remove the hoods from the rest of the hostages and cut their legs free.

He was dragged to his right, into a large open space within the boathouse. At one side of it was a long table that Jake Han was sitting at, finishing putting back together a .45 automatic.

This is what John had heard while he was still hooded and bound. He had known it was a .45 just by the sounds of the stripping and cleaning process.

On the table in front of Jake Han were the bulletproof vests and weapons The Brotherhood had taken from their hostages. Jake had the .45 automatic pistol he'd just put back together in his right hand and another .45 automatic placed separately on the table, just in front of his left hand, which he now picked up.

As John was frog-marched into the space in front of him, Jake had something to say to him.

"Hey John, I hear you're a big John Woo fan."

Burnum and Jeff Han stopped pushing John towards the spot where they wanted him, temporarily, and turned him around to face Jake, so that he could reply.

John saw no point in denying this or being awkward. Besides, if he was about to be killed and these were to be his last words, he wasn't going to shuffle off this mortal coil having falsely denied his love of John Woo.

The end is important in all things.

"Yep."

Upon receiving this response, Jake raised up the two .45 automatics in his hands and aimed them at John.

"A Better Tomorrow motherfucker!"

Jake pulled the hammers back on the pistols with his thumbs and stared through John with deadly intent. After a few seconds though, he uncocked the hammers of the guns and laughed, setting them down on the table in front of him.

"You just shit yourself mate," he laughingly informed John.

"Whatever dickhead. A Better Tomorrow II is better anyway."

Jake Han did not agree, but he wasn't going to get into a debate over their slightly differing opinions on John Woo's masterpieces of heroic bloodshed cinema. He nodded to Burnum and his brother Jeff to continue with putting John in position.

They marched him over to the other side of the room and spun him round so that he was facing Jake, who remained seated at the table. Burnum then kicked his right foot hard into the back of John's left knee, dropping him down to the floor on his knees.

The rest of the members of the two Brotherhood chapters walked the other prisoners over to the area directly in front of the table, where Jake Han remained sitting, having removed their cloth hoods and cut their feet free. They were all then forced down on their knees in a line, facing John, with their wrists still bound behind their backs.

Once they had everyone in position, a couple of the Brotherhood members pulled out their guns and stood guard at either end of the line.

The rest of them moved over to the side of this clear area of the boathouse. They had effectively formed a human wall at one side, facing the metal wall opposite, which was around twenty metres in front of them.

There was another metal wall a few feet behind John, and he had Jeff Han and Burnum standing over him.

Behind Jake Han, sat at the table, was a railing and beyond that was the area of the boathouse where the water came in, with a fifty foot luxury yacht floating and rocking gently with the lapping salt water. John could see the name of the yacht painted on the side of it; it was called the All For One.

He also noticed that beside the railing, seemingly in place to be put on the boat and taken for disposal in the ocean, were the dead bodies of Nate and Poots. Nate's body had been placed on top of Poots and John felt sure that they would all soon be part of a pile of corpses, thrown callously beside the yacht.

At this point, John wanted more than anything to just get on that boat with Lisa and Blair and sail out of this hellish situation and on out to sea. He wanted out.

There seemed little hope of that though, as Kate parted the human wall at the side of this area of the boathouse and took centre stage, right in the middle of the space between John and the other prisoners, and turned to face her troops.

"Well done guys. We now own this city!"

This brought a cheer from all of the members of The Brotherhood, even those from the Perth chapter.

"So, you all know about our brother Steven Watkins."

The crowd of Brotherhood members took on a more sombre tone as soon as this name was mentioned.

"His friends in the Sydney chapter knew him simply as Stevie or Steve-o. We will all remember him as the first martyr of the Australian Brotherhood.

You are all aware that last weekend he was kidnapped, tortured, murdered and his body disposed of by our enemies.

What some of you may not know is that those enemies are the very scumbags we have tied up on their knees before us. Believe me when I say we are going to make them pay.

Let's show these fuckers what happens to you when you fuck with The Brotherhood!"

This brought a bloodthirsty cheer from the line of gang members looking on. The four members of the Brotherhood standing over the prisoners at opposite sides of this part of the boathouse also joined in the cheering, as well as Jake Han, who was still sat at the table covered in weapons and bulletproof vests.

John was shocked. If it was at all possible, their situation had just got more bleak. Any remote possibility of even a small degree of mercy for him, Blair and the other gang members was surely gone.

John's mind was racing.

He had hoped that either Kate wasn't aware that this Brotherhood member - who he now knew was called Steven Watkins - was missing yet, that she knew he was missing and blamed some other enemies of The Brotherhood, or that she just wasn't sure what had happened to him. His hopes had just been completely dashed.

Had Kate known what they'd done all along? Had she been watching their every move the whole time? Did she let them take Steven Watkins, torture him and kill him?

Had she allowed the situation to happen and play out as it had, just to make a martyr and create this scenario, which she could use to her advantage and boost her power within this new incarnation of The Brotherhood?

If she'd known all along, if she'd been watching their every move and allowed them to torture and kill one of her gang members just to enhance her own position, then she was probably perfect as a leader for this sickening drug gang, thought John.

This was exactly the kind of thing the two previous leaders, Doug and Simon, would have done. They had been totally ruthless and completely selfish and self-serving, while paying lip service to ideas of loyalty and brotherhood.

"He may be a cunt and an enemy of The Brotherhood, but we couldn't have taken Sydney without the famous John Kennedy and his little gang of super friends.

Please give them a big round of applause!"

An enthusiastic round of applause, accompanied with laughter, was the response from The Brotherhood members to this request.

Kate then turned to face John, who was looking on from the position he was in, down on his knees, before continuing.

"Thanks John, you didn't let me down. You really are a natural born killer. Unfortunately, you have to die.

If the last eight months have taught me anything, it's that you cannot be allowed to live. You're a fucking menace to drug dealers everywhere. And anyone who fucks with The Brotherhood has to die in a world of pain.

Steven Watkins hadn't been in The Brotherhood for long, but he was one of us. He was our brother. You and your fucking gang of wannabes gave him an awful death.

Now it's payback time and every single one of you is going to die at our hands. You're going to die really fucking badly and we are all going to really fucking enjoy it."

"You fucking lying bitch!" shouted John.

This brought him an immediate punishment blow to the back of the head with Burnum's quartz tipped club. John made a point of not showing any pain, as blood tricked down the back of his head on to his neck.

"And you John are a name-caller. You are right though; I am a lying bitch. Fucking sue me, you stupid cunt."

Kate turned one hundred and eighty degrees to face the rest of her prisoners, in a row on their knees, looking up at her.

"Blair and the rest of you chumps, take a look at what you could have won. This place is what I like to call our smuggling and murder hub.

We can bring in all the drugs and guns we need and bring out all the bodies of people we don't. It's fucking perfect and this whole country is about to get its arse fucked by The Brotherhood."

This remark brought a number of sniggers from the watching members of the two chapters of The Brotherhood.

There was nothing John, Lisa, Blair or any of his surviving gang members could say in response, so they just continued to listen to Kate make her big leadership speech. She was clearly using all this to further consolidate her position of power within The Brotherhood in Australia.

"There's no fucking way I'd let any of you bitches into The Brotherhood. Even if you hadn't killed Stevie, you little faggots aren't Brotherhood material.

Lisa has no Brotherhood blood on her hands though. Maybe she could still be of some use to us; she could make me cups of tea and I could use her as my fucking footstool."

Kate saying this made Lisa's blood boil, but she knew better than to shout out a response. She had a gun pointed at her head and she believed that she'd mostly outlived her usefulness to Kate and The Brotherhood.

"Right then, without further a do, let's start the killing."

Chapter Thirty-Seven

The prisoners on their knees, facing John, at the other side of the clear part of the boathouse, were lined up with Lisa to his left as he looked at them, then Blair, then Mack and then the other two surviving members of Blair's gang, Smitty and Jason.

Six members of The Brotherhood grabbed Smitty and Jason from either side and behind, with three of them taking hold of each one. They then dragged both of them into the centre of this area and put them in position, down on their knees, facing John, with all six Brotherhood members remaining with the two prisoners, holding them firmly in place.

"Let the games begin!" Kate announced to the crowd with gusto.

Jake Han stood up from behind the table and made his way into the centre, so that he was standing over Smitty and Jason, with his back to John. Jeff Han then made his way from his position, standing behind John, to join his brother.

Burnum made a point of poking John hard in the back of the head with the sharp tip of his club, just to let him know he was still there.

Although John was trying desperately to think of an escape plan, at this point Burnum didn't have anything to worry about. His guard duties would be easy.

To John, there seemed to be no way out.

Jake and Jeff both pulled out their Rambo knives in tandem, ready for action.

"You go first mate," said Jake.

"No, after you," replied Jeff, as they joked around with traditional manners, while preparing to commit two cold-blooded murders.

"Okay, hold him still and stick his head out," Jake said to the three members of The Brotherhood holding Jason in place on his knees.

The three Brotherhood members followed his instructions as best they could, with Jason now doing everything he could to squirm his body free. There was little he could realistically do to change the outcome, however; he was going to die.

Jake took a few steps away from Jason in the direction of John, taking the opportunity to give him a wink and a smile. He then spun around, took a short run up, jumped into the air, with his knife gripped in both hands and the blade pointing downwards, and slammed the knife down hard through the top of Jason's head.

The sound of the crack and crunch of the impact on his skull echoed around the metal boathouse, as Jason's lifeless body was allowed to slump forwards. There wasn't a lot of blood, considering a death blow to the head had just been delivered with a large knife.

The three members of The Brotherhood who had been holding him in place made their way back over to the side of the clear area, to once again stand in line with the other members. As the body lay flat on the ground, Jake Han knelt down, yanked his Rambo knife out of Jason's head and wiped the bloody blade on Jason's t-shirt until it was clean. He then stood up again, slid the knife back into its sheath and enthusiastically gave a high five to his brother Jeff.

"First time, every time!" he shouted.

It was clear to John, as he knelt there watching this horror show, that Kate was taking a leaf out of Simon's book by consolidating her power in this way, but she had obviously learned from his mistakes as well.

She was giving the members of The Brotherhood from both chapters a show and cementing her position as overall leader, but at the same time she was not giving their prisoners any chance to fight back and upset her plans.

"Fuck you two! Fuck you all, you fuckin' pussies!" shouted Smitty, aghast at what had just happened to Jason and knowing that he was next.

"What a foul mouth," said Jeff Han to his brother, at a volume that everyone could hear.

"Yeah, I don't like his mouth," replied Jake.

"Fuck it bro, I don't like his whole fucking face."

Jake Han smiled back at his brother, as Jeff took a firm grasp of the handle of his Rambo knife in his right hand and grabbed Smitty firmly by the hair at the front of his head with his left. Three Brotherhood members were already holding Smitty securely in place, but now he couldn't move his head at all.

Jeff then began thrusting his knife as hard as he could, in and out of Smitty's face. He was in a frenzy, so that it seemed as if the knife was moving in and out of Smitty's head at least once every second. Blood was flying out everywhere, in large splashes, as Smitty's face gradually became an unrecognisable mess.

By the time Jeff Han stopped the frantic stabbing, gasping for breath and hanging the knife down with his right hand from his exhausted arm, Smitty had lost his face and his life.

Jeff's clothes had been sprayed with blood and as he stepped back, he wiped the blood from his knife on to his trousers, obviously long past caring about getting bloodstains on them.

He put his knife back in the leather sheath hanging from his belt, as the three members of The Brotherhood who had been holding Smitty in place dropped his faceless body to the ground, into a large pool of his own blood.

Kate made her way back into the centre of the murder area, as Jake and Jeff Han walked towards the spot where John was kneeling. They took up positions standing behind him, beside Burnum.

The three members of The Brotherhood who had been holding Smitty remained where they were, as Kate once again addressed the crowd of gang members.

"Right everyone, I hope you enjoyed that!"

There was an enthusiastic round of cheering and applause from the members of The Brotherhood.

"Okay, if everyone could pitch in and help clear these bodies over beside the boat and clean up all this blood, then we can get on with the next round of executions."

NEIL WALKER

Chapter Thirty-Eight

The three members of The Brotherhood who'd been holding Smitty in place for his brutal murder had stayed in the centre of the killing zone of the boathouse. They were joined by most of the other Brotherhood members, to move the dead bodies of Jason and Smitty over to the designated spot beside the boat.

The remaining members of The Brotherhood then cleaned up the mess. The exceptions were those guarding the prisoners, with two of them maintaining their positions standing at either end of the now shortened prisoner line of Lisa, Blair and Mack, with their guns trained on them.

Burnum and the Han brothers stayed where they were, in place behind John.

The area was soon clean and clear again, and Kate once more walked into the middle to address the crowd. This time she had a small sword in her right hand.

"This is my estoca," she said.

She held the sword up in the air so they could all get a good look, before lowering it to her side and continuing.

"I first saw bullfighting when I was a teenager in Marbella and I've been in love with it ever since. Some people say it's cruel to the bulls; they can fuck off.

It's mostly a man's game, but there have been a few female bullfighters - the exceptions that prove the rule. My favourite, and one of my heroines, was Cristina Sánchez de Pablos.

I would love to have been a bullfighter like her. I even used to practice my finishing technique with my estoca.

I'll give you a little demonstration. Could a few of you bring out the next one?"

The first three members of The Brotherhood to react made their way over to the line of prisoners, where Mack was next in line to be murdered. They picked him up, dragged him into the centre of the execution area and shoved him down on his knees, while Kate just stood there, spinning her sword in her hand.

"The killer blow is called an estocada," she continued. "You've got to do it quickly and cleanly, or the crowd hate it and they boo the matador. It's all about one strike and a quick death.

Now, with a bull you go for the spinal chord. With a human, I like to go for jugular. If the matador manages a fast kill, with a single strike, the crowd goes crazy.

Then the matador cuts off trophies from the corpse and throws them out to the crowd. So I hope I get a big cheer for a clean kill!"

The crowd cheered to show their agreement and enthusiasm, as well as their excitement to witness what was about to happen.

"Hold his head up and back. Keep him nice and still," were her instructions to the three members of The Brotherhood holding Mack on his knees in front of her.

Blair and John just looked on from either side of the killing area, on their knees with their hands bound behind their backs. They wished they could help and stop this grotesque spectacle from unfolding, but they were both completely powerless to do anything.

Lisa was horrified at what she was witnessing and was trying desperately to think of anything she could do or say to intervene and stop this blood-soaked madness. Soon it would be the end for John and probably for her too.

Kate stood still, aiming her sword down at Mack, for what seemed to Blair, John and Lisa to be an eternity, before she launched forward, stabbing it as hard as she could straight into his jugular. She then pulled it out in a single powerful motion, stepping back and to the side, to avoid the jet of blood that came spraying out.

This prompted a huge cheer and round of applause from all the watching members of The Brotherhood.

Kate took the accolades, as the three members of The Brotherhood who had been holding Mack in place let his dead body slump down on its face and made their way back to the side of the clear part of the boathouse, to rejoin the row of enthusiastic watching gang members.

Kate then knelt down and pulled out an ejector knife from the inside of her Dr. Martens boot, before flicking out the blade. She stepped in closer to the body, leaned down on the back of Mack's head with her right knee, and began slicing off his right ear.

Once she had the bloody ear cut off and held in her left hand, she threw it to the crowd, who were standing at the side of the action. One of them caught it and this brought another cheer from the membership of The Brotherhood, as Kate went to work cutting off the other ear.

After she'd removed the other ear and thrown it to the crowd in the same way, the members of her gang were once again instructed to clear away the body and the blood. This did not take long and it was soon time for the main event.

Kate took centre stage once more, now basking in the glow of adoration from these bloodthirsty gang members.

The noisy murmur from The Brotherhood members died down, as Kate began to address them again.

"Usually the matador doesn't go in for the kill against the bull right away. There is a team of other bullfighters who tenderise it first, before the matador finishes the job.

Today's prize bull is John Kennedy. You all know who he is and I'm sure you all can't wait to see the cunt die; am I right?"

This brought a roar of noisy agreement from the crowd.

"Me too. I'm fucking wet just thinking about it. But I can't kill him too quickly. He made the previous leaders of The Brotherhood, Simon and Doug, suffer and die slowly, so I have to make sure he goes out in a world of hurt.

Then I'm going to skewer him and cut off some trophies. I'm sure you'll all want one."

Another cheer went up in response to this.

"There'll be plenty to go round. I'm going to take his balls for myself, after I slice them off. I'll keep them in a jam jar beside my bed."

Kate, while still addressing this eager audience, turned to face John. She wanted to look him in the eye as she explained his fate.

"Johnny Boy, it's time to start dying. We're going to tenderise the fuck out of you before I finish the job. In the end, you'll be thanking me when I step up to kill you.

I have seen what you can do though. I watched you take Dave apart in The Casa in Manchester. But this time I've got your bitch.

You are dead and Blair is dead, after I've let him watch you die first. You're such a father figure to that little prick; or at the very least a big brother figure, or maybe a gay uncle or whatever.

Lisa might get to live. You see, we've become gal pals since we've been living together. Like I said before, I might even keep her around as my tea girl and footstool.

Her life is in your hands, dickhead. If you start ripping out throats and dropping bodies, she's fucking dead, after she spends about a fortnight on the rape train. You can defend yourself a bit, just to keep us entertained, but if you fuck around, it's on her.

Do you understand?"

John nodded with a look of resignation on his face that told her he was ready to go along with whatever she said, if there was any chance it would save Lisa.

"Okay, Jake, Jeff, Burnum; tool up and cut him free. It's time to begin the John Kennedy murder fiesta!"

Chapter Thirty-Nine

The crowd were cheering and clapping in time, as John stood there topless, having had his t-shirt removed at Kate's insistence. He was facing Burnum and the Han brothers, and was ready to meet his end.

Jake and Jeff were each wielding a baseball bat, while Burnum was holding his trusty quartz tipped, fire hardened, traditional Aboriginal club.

The only thing John cared about in this moment was Lisa. He knew he was finished, but he had to give Lisa a chance of staying alive.

He would take all the punishment these guys could dish out and then let Kate finish him off like a matador. To do this, he would have to control all of his instincts, natural reflexes and reactions, to hold back from killing or badly hurting his opponents.

As his three eager adversaries were spinning their weapons in their hands, playing to the audience, a loud screaming voice cut through the crowd noise. It was Lisa.

"John, please no! I love you John!" she yelled out with tears in her eyes.

She had thrown herself down and to the side as she shouted, so that she ended up lying across Blair's thighs, as he knelt beside her to the left.

Ray - the one remaining member of The Brotherhood who was supposed to be guarding Lisa and Blair - hadn't even really been paying attention. He had just been standing there, pointing his gun down at the two prisoners, but watching the build-up to this fervently anticipated fight.

It was only when he heard Lisa screaming - over the sounds of the crowd - that he spun back around, to see that she was out of position.

Ray laughed at her desperate shouting, as did the rest of this barbaric group of Brotherhood members. They then immediately turned their focus back to the fight.

Ray did the same, after he had sat Lisa back up on her knees to watch John's demise.

John looked over at Lisa and Blair and he immediately knew what was happening. While no one else had given Lisa's actions a second thought, John knew she had a plan.

She had remembered about Blair's belt; his novelty belt buckle, which concealed a knife that could be popped out for quick use. The Brotherhood had thoroughly searched all of their prisoners for weapons and removed any they'd found, but they hadn't taken away Blair's belt.

John could see that Lisa had managed to get her tied hands on the knife. It was apparent to him from looking at Blair's belt from across the killing floor of the boathouse, but only because he had seen the knife taken off it before and knew exactly what he was looking for.

He now knew that all he had to do was give this crowd of savage killers, collectively high on the sights and sounds of limitless violence, a show they couldn't take their eyes off, to distract them while Lisa tried to cut herself and Blair free.

They were still in a difficult situation, in a boathouse in the middle of nowhere, surrounded by the armed members of both the Sydney and Perth chapters of The Brotherhood. Now the three of them had a chance to survive, however, thanks to Lisa's quick thinking.

His three attackers came at him at once and he had to use low front kicks to keep them from getting too close, as they rained in blows with their weapons. He was caught around the legs with the baseball bats and on his right arm by the quartz tipped club, which drew blood with a stinging, razor-sharp strike.

He couldn't let them hurt him too badly, as he would still have to try and fight his way out of this place, if Blair and Lisa could get loose.

As Jake Han swung in his baseball bat with both hands, for another low swipe, John stamped down on it with his left foot, and as the end of it crashed against the concrete floor, he used it as a springboard to launch forward with a right knee to Jake's head.

He came down with a spinning back fist to his right, catching Jeff Han hard on the right side of his face. As both Han brothers stumbled back, dazed, Burnum launched himself at John with his deadly club.

John was caught again on the right forearm with the sharp quartz, as he defended himself, before parrying the club with his left hand and head-butting Burnum as hard as he could on the bridge of his nose, breaking it.

As Burnum stumbled back, with tears in his eyes and blood streaming out of his nose, John looked over at Lisa and Blair to find that they were ready to go.

All three of his opponents seemed to gather themselves and come at John simultaneously. Burnum was going to get there first, and the only thought in John's mind now was that it was time to finish them and rely on Blair to back him up.

John dodged right quickly, as Burnum stabbed at his face with the quartz tip of his club, before grabbing his forearm with his left hand, taking hold of the middle of the club with his right and snatching it out of Burnum's grip. He stabbed it with incredible force, as hard as he could, into Burnum's right eye and upwards into his brain.

John then spun around to engage the Han brothers in combat, as Burnum dropped to the ground dead behind him.

John bobbed left, to slip a baseball bat blow from Jeff Han, before pulling Jeff's Rambo knife out of the sheath on his belt and raising it up to slit his throat in one swift motion.

Warm blood sprayed out of the deep wound over the side of John's face and on to his shoulder and bare torso.

He then used his left hand to quickly place Jeff's head in the way of Jake's impending baseball bat blow at the last second. John let Jeff Han's limp body drop to the ground, as Jake's bat impacted on his dying brother's head.

At this point, John just stepped in close to Jake Han and stabbed the Rambo knife in his hand powerfully upwards through his head. There was a slam of impact, followed by a crunch as John twisted the long, thick blade.

Blood streamed down his arm as he kept him skewered by the head like this with his right hand, to use him as a human shield, as gunfire began to ring out and Jake Han's lifeless eyes stared ahead into nothingness.

After Lisa had cut her hands free behind her back, she had swiftly and discreetly cut the cable tie around Blair's wrists. Blair had stabbed Ray - the member of The Brotherhood who had been tasked with guarding him and Lisa - in the throat with the knife Lisa had removed from his belt and had taken the Beretta .9mm automatic pistol he'd been pointing at them as his next weapon of choice.

He was now firing on the line of gang members at the side of the fight area with this pistol, hitting a number of them in quick succession, before they could even draw their weapons.

Lisa moved quickly to get the bulletproof vests from the table, while John dragged his upright human shield, by the handle of the knife lodged through his head, towards Blair and Lisa.

Those members of The Brotherhood that were not hit in the initial round of gunfire ran as fast as they could into the other area of the boathouse, to seek shelter and take up firing positions. Kate had so far managed to avoid being shot.

Lisa put a bulletproof vest on as swiftly as she could and then put one on Blair, as he kept shooting. When John made it over to her, he dropped Jake Han's body to the ground and grabbed her powerfully in his arms, throwing her down to the floor at the side of the table.

He grabbed a couple of extra bulletproof vests from the table and placed them on top of her, before putting one on himself, with split second efficiency.

Gunfire had started being returned from multiple angles, as The Brotherhood fought back. John picked up Blair's own Beretta .9mm pistol from the table and threw it to him, just as the one he had been using ran out of bullets.

He dropped it from his right hand, caught the one John had thrown in his left and kept firing. This meant that there was no let up in gunfire from their side of the boathouse.

John picked up his own two .45 automatic pistols, one in each hand.

He opened fire with speed and accuracy from both guns simultaneously and, given the limited cover available in the boathouse and the fact that the members of The Brotherhood did not have bulletproof vests on, those that had remained alive started dropping like flies, under well-aimed gunfire from both John and Blair.

Blair was also a great shot and it was clear that both he and John were far superior with guns to any of their rivals. As the Brotherhood numbers fell away, John saw Kate make a break for the door.

She got out unharmed and John shouted instruction to Blair.

"Finish them!"

He then bolted after her, almost ignoring the gunfire that they were still receiving, as he ran the gauntlet through the boathouse to the sliding metal door, firing from both pistols as he charged for the exit.

Blair used these few seconds of cover and distraction provided by John to step over to the table, drop the now empty Beretta to the ground and pick up two fully loaded Glock 17 automatics, one in each hand.

Blair opened fire on the remaining members of The Brotherhood from both guns simultaneously, just as John made it to the metal door of the boathouse. He somehow made it out through the door without being hit and all of his enemies inside the boathouse were too engrossed in the gunfight and under too much heavy fire from Blair to think about following him.

Once outside, John shouted after Kate, who was running away.

"Kate!"

She stopped in her tracks when she heard his voice and turned to face him. She had a gun in her hand, but it was by her side and John had the drop on her, with his two .45 automatic pistols raised to fire.

"I would tell you to go to hell, but I don't believe in that shit," he said.

He pulled the triggers on both pistols at once.

As the hammers clicked down and no gunshots ensued, John was hit by the horrible realisation that he was out of bullets. Kate laughed, before raising up the .45 automatic pistol she was holding and aiming it at his head, so as to avoid the bulletproof vest.

"We're both going to hell Johnny Boy. Let's just hope we get good seats when we get there," she said.

She smiled as she pulled the trigger on her nemesis John.

John couldn't believe his luck, as the hammer clicked down on her pistol and she too had run out of bullets. They had both lost track of how many shots they'd fired, in the boathouse gun battle, and would now have to finish this without firearms.

Kate charged towards John, throwing her pistol at his head as she leapt into the air, launching a left front kick to his chest and hooking a right side kick at his neck, before landing back down on her feet.

John had been stunned, by almost being shot to death, and distracted by the .45 automatic pistol nearly hitting him in the face. He had barely managed to drop his pistols before the kicks were impacting on him.

Now he was ready though.

He moved forward, blocking her incoming low right kick with his left arm, before catching her on the chin with a right uppercut and following it up with a flurry of straight punches to her face. She didn't manage to get her hands up in time and all of the punches landed, knocking her to the ground.

John just stood there, allowing her time to get up. He took off his bulletproof vest and let it drop to the dust beneath him, as his opponent began getting to her feet.

As she did so, she reached into her Dr. Martens boot and produced her ejector knife, flicking out the blade and charging at John with it. He managed to parry the firm and powerful knife strike, which was aimed at his throat, just enough so that it instead stabbed him in the flesh just above his collarbone.

With his left arm, he knocked her right arm away from the imbedded knife and with his right hand he pulled it out in one hard motion.

Then, with a second even firmer motion, he stabbed the blade into her throat. He pulled it out and blood squirted back at him, over his already blood-soaked face and bare torso, as he stepped away to watch her fall to the ground and let the life drain from her.

As he stood over her, watching her blood pour out and sink into the dust, he could hear that the gunfire inside had stopped.

He looked around to see Blair emerge at the door of the boathouse, holding a pistol by his side with his right hand and giving a thumbs-up signal with his left.

John smiled and sighed in disbelief as the realisation hit him; they were alive. They had gone right to edge of annihilation, but they'd actually managed to survive.

Chapter Forty

It had only been two years, though it seemed like so much longer, only two years since he first returned from Australia, only two years since it all began. Now it was finally over.

They'd seen no need to travel to the boat Blair had previously arranged, with The Brotherhood's yacht - the All For One - sitting right there, ready to go. Besides, Blair had told them that the All For One was far superior to the boat he'd organised anyway.

It would have also been risky, after this all-out massacre, to do anything other than get out of Australia immediately. John and Lisa were already being sought by the police, without adding all these bodies to their wanted poster.

Blair had been a little worried that they would encounter the coast guard or the Australian Navy, but he let John and Lisa know when they were far enough out to sea that he felt they were safe.

Fortunately, there was a medical kit on the boat, so Lisa had been tending to John's injuries while Blair had been sailing them to freedom.

They had a decent supply of strong prescription painkillers and drinks on the boat as well. Once Lisa had finished patching him up, John had taken four tramadol capsules and three 30mg co-codamol tablets, washed down with a couple of bottles of Lucozade and a few swigs of whiskey. This was more than the recommended dose of both medications, plus you were not supposed to mix them with alcohol, but John had long since stopped taking such recommendations seriously.

When all the painkillers, glucose and alcohol kicked in, he perked up quite dramatically, although he would still require a bit of a recovery period when they got to Papua New Guinea. He confirmed with Lisa that she had not been harmed while she'd been a prisoner of Kate and The Brotherhood, which was a huge relief to him.

He then left Lisa sitting at the back of the boat for a while and went up to speak to Blair at the front. Blair was steering the yacht and doing his sailor thing.

"You got your passport and bank stuff mate?" John asked.

"Oh yes," replied Blair, tapping the side pocket of his combat trousers. "You got your passports and bank stuff?"

"Yep," replied John, tapping the same pocket on his own combat trousers.

"Crime pays, eh mate," Blair joked.

"You really still believe that Blair?"

"Fuck no. It wasn't worth it, but at least we're alive and we've got a few bucks to start over."

"Yeah man, I agree. I want to undo it all, but you can't can you? At least the money will help us get a fresh start."

"I know mate. I can't believe everything that's happened and I'd love to go back and do it all differently."

Blair paused for a few seconds, before speaking again.

"Oh by the way, I got my HIV test back this week. I got so caught up in the drug war, I forgot to bloody tell you."

John had not wanted to ask him about this, since the rape, but he'd known that he was getting tested.

"Well mate?"

"Negative. I couldn't fucking believe it. I still have to get tested again in another six months, but I had myself dead and buried. Then I'm in that boathouse thinking, it doesn't fucking matter that I'm HIV negative. I'm a dead man anyway. I mean, how the fuck are we still alive?"

"Fuck knows mate. It's all still a bit of a blur. Great news about the LucozAIDS though," said John, trying to lighten the mood and inspired by the Lucozade he'd been drinking.

"LucozAIDS?" Blair laughingly questioned.

"Yeah; another one for my jokes in bad taste collection. I can't laugh myself though."

John smiled and then continued.

"My knife wound only hurts when I laugh."

This made Blair laugh even more.

"What are we going to do about the money and drugs in the storage unit that we took from the Greeks and The Hatchet Mob?" asked John.

"When we get where we're going, I'll call my cousin in Perth and ask him to do a bandit run from west to east and pick them up for us. He still feels bad about Lisa getting snatched on the way to his place - even though it wasn't his fault - so I reckon I can talk him into it. Plus I'll tell him he can keep the drugs and sell them if he wants."

"You don't want to sell them when you get back to Oz?"

"No way," replied Blair, "no more drug dealing for me. I'm out of that shit for good."

"Sounds like the way forward mate."

"I think I'll stick with you pair for a bit, when we get to Papua New Guinea, if that's okay? I don't want to cramp your style or anything."

"You're welcome to stay with us for as long as you want mate. Travel around the fucking world with us if you fancy it," said John.

"I might just take you up on that," Blair replied with a smile.

John made his way back to Lisa, who was still sitting at the stern of the boat, staring at the red sunset glistening on the water.

He popped open the side pocket of his combat trousers and took out their passports, getting Lisa's attention by tapping her shoulder with hers.

He sat down beside her, as she opened it up and took a look inside.

"I'm Mrs. Pamela Susan Douglas am I?"

"Yes. And I'm Mr. James Douglas."

"Oh yeah? Won't I need a ring?" she asked with a wry smile.

"Don't worry, I'll put a ring on your finger when we get where we're going."

Lisa felt a warm glow of happy realisation at what this could mean. She handed the passport back to John. He put both passports safely back into the pocket of his combats and joined Lisa in staring out at the dying red sun dancing on the water, as the magic hour drew to a close.

"So, is this the part where we sail off into the sunset?" asked Lisa.

John took a moment to look around him and reflect on everything, while Lisa waited for an answer.

He put his hand on his pocket, once again reassuring himself that he had their passports and the items needed to access the money to start their new life on him.

He looked across at Blair, as he sailed them to freedom, and once again at the magnificent and beautiful sunset.

John finally turned and looked deep into the eyes of the love of his life, before giving her his reply.

"Yeah, I think it is."

THE END

DRUG GANG TAKEDOWN

I hope you have enjoyed this novel. Please take a moment to leave a review on Amazon.

Reviews are a critical factor in the success of any novel and are a powerful buying tool to help readers find the right book. As an author, I really appreciate it when readers review my work and I very much enjoy reading their thoughts.

To leave a review, just go to the Amazon page for Drug Gang Takedown and then click on 'write a customer review'.

Many thanks,

Neil Walker

ABOUT THE AUTHOR

Neil Walker is the bestselling Belfast author of hard-hitting crime fiction. His works include the acclaimed crime thriller Drug Gang and its sequel Drug Gang Vengeance.

Both of these controversial bestsellers are part of the Drug Gang Trilogy and are set in the drug dealing underworld of Manchester, Sydney and Belfast in the early 2000s.

The third and final Drug Gang novel, Drug Gang Takedown, was published in January 2019 and quickly became a bestseller.

To learn more, visit the author's social media pages:

twitter.com/neilwalkerwrote

facebook.com/neilwalkerauthor

instagram.com/neilwalkerauthor

#DrugGang
#DrugGangVengeance
#DrugGangTakedown
#DrugGangTrilogy

Printed in Great Britain
by Amazon